WILL'S GARDEN

Lee Maracle

Theytus Books

Library and Archives Canada Cataloguing in Publication

Maracle, Lee, 1950-
Will's garden / Lee Maracle. -- Rev. ed.

ISBN 978-1-894778-59-6

I. Title.

PS8576.A6175W44 2008   jC813'.54   C2008-901387-5

Cover Painting: "Village Boys" by Jim Logan
Cover and text redesign: Suzanne Bates
Copy-Editing: Leanne Flett-Kruger

Printed in Canada

Printed on Ancient Forest Friendly 100% post consumer fibre paper.

On behalf on Theytus Books, we would like to acknowledge the support of the following:
We acknowledge the financial support of the Government of Canada through the Book
Publishing Industry Development Program (BPIDP) for our publishing activities.
We acknowledge the support of the Canada Council for the Arts which last year invest-
ed $20.1 million in writing and publishing throughout Canada.
Nous remercions de son soutien le Conseil des Arts du Canada, qui a investi 20,1 mil-
lions de dollars l'an dernier dans les lettres et l'édition à travers le Canada.
We acknowledge the support of the Province of British Columbia through the British
Columbia Arts Council.

BRITISH COLUMBIA
ARTS COUNCIL

Canada Council
for the Arts
Conseil des Arts
du Canada

Patrimoine
canadien
Canadian
Heritage

Acknowledgements

Will's Garden came about as a result of having received
the JT Stewart Award for "culturally appropriate writing",
which turned out to be a sum of money and included
a month all-paid retreat at Hedgebrook.
I wish to thank the jurists who chose me, and the women
at Hedgebrook who made the draft of this novel possible.
I also wish to thank the editors at Theytus Books for their
tedious job of combing through and rendering the
manuscript a smooth and lovely read.

Prelude

I'm laying in the dark. It's a gentle quiet dark. Ol' Gramma Moon is splitting the darkness in my room with pale blue shafts of light, dividing the field of vision into columns of blind spots and clarity. The light is poking through dark clouds. Night opens me up to dreamtime. At night when the moon wrestles with dark fluffy clouds like she's doing now, I feel like I can remember backwards and forwards. I can remember how it felt to bustle about the beach loading a big canoe a century ago. I can remember digging pits, preparing *oolichans*, watching them transform from candlefish to grease; I can almost feel the steady warm from hot rocks as the little fish slowly melt. I can remember crawling up the Coquihalla pass, pack on my back, setting up camp on the hillsides, building shelters and picking blueberries. I watch the images of our women in my mind, bodies swaying to the berry picking songs they sing as they pick.

I imagine which young woman might end up being my life-long partner. I feel the excitement of seeing her for the first time and knowing, just knowing; this is the one. Her hips move with personality; there is a basket covering her back that begins just between her shoulder blades and ends at the small space in the center of her waist. Her body is sultry; she is so graceful she looks like she glides uphill; she's not stumbling and crawling like the rest of us, and then I chide myself. I tell myself to behave. Alone in the bedroom is not a good time for my thoughts to run in that direction, too risky.

I know the pictures are old, but I make-believe I am in them. Snippets I call them. I don't remember when I first started seeing snippets in the skirt of the moon, but it feels like I have been seeing them forever.

Raven's wings are spreading out, not an ordinary black crow like you see today squawking from the telephone wires, but old time Raven, the one that shape shifts, calls up the rain and can flood the world—the one that bit off a piece of the moon and built the earth—a powerhouse Raven. She can sink whole territories if she wants. I mean, the Raven who is in charge.

Raven is at the top of Cheam Mountain. Screaming Skull is having a quiet conversation with her.

"The Eagles will return and half of them will die," Screaming Skull says.

"Why?" I wonder. Whoosh... Raven's gone and an old woman is standing there.

"You're too old to be asking why," this old granny says.

"Too old?" I parrot the critical part of her statement by way of a question.

"Um-umph. 'Why' is what three-year-olds ask. You want to be wondering what it means to you to have Eagle return." Floop. She is gone. Whoosh and Raven is back. She spreads her wings again. Screaming Skull is quiet. Raven's answer was like a warning. I stare at Screaming Skull wondering what the return of Eagle really does mean. Eagle stories whirl inside my mind picking up speed. Eagle called the Spirit World together for a meeting, and poof, next thing you know we all take on physical form and endure thousands of years of trail-busting history. I stop there. My recalling Raven becoming the old woman, then flying off again had interrupted my original train of stories. I return to them; that gets me to wondering in what century am I chasing these moonbeam movies.

There is no one else but me on this mountain. I look around. No roads. The land is all brush, berries and trees. The trees are young. I can tell because they are spindly. I know Cedar. She can reach huge proportions. She can grow to be as big as them Sequoias, as long as disease, fire or man doesn't kill her. The only difference between Sequoia and Cedar is that Cedar can get sick and die or burn in a forest fire; Sequoia cannot. Sequoia has to be killed by humans. This realization now moves me to awe. The thought of killing something that powerful is terrifying. Sequoia has a place in my hereafter. I would not want to be one of the guys who killed one and had to go home telling that story. These trees are only three inches thick–babies. They are growing in neat rows, so men must have planted them. They look constrained by this unnecessary order like kids in a classroom. They are tense. I can feel the tension. I know Cheam was planted in the 60s, they must be thirty years old today. Beyond that I have no idea what year it is. Wait a minute; the picture is changing. There is my Gramma and my mom sitting with my aunt Josie in my aunt's kitchen.

"They are pinning up Cheam," Aunt Josie says, laughing her gutsy, pretty-sounding Sto: loh laugh. This laugh means she's laughing at some men's antics. This laugh gets the gleam going in the old guys' eyes if they hear it. Usually they don't get to hear it. She reserves it for herself, the women and small children, so if some old guy hears it, it is because he was secretly listening in on Josie's conversation. It always feels somewhat sneaky and happily wicked to hear this laugh, like it is a secret between us kids and Aunt Josie.

"You're kidding right? They aren't really?" my mom says.

"I kid you not," Josic answers her. She is real serious. "Damn fools."

I want to ask them what they are talking about—but I don't. I do the Indian thing of waiting for the story to unfold. I know it'll happen. Our women tell stories in a certain way. The back end point or result is thrown out first. If that gets the listener's attention, the speaker tells the story; front to back, otherwise the information just dies. It has something to do with courtesy. If no one is interested, no one is bored by having to listen to the story. Josie has their attention so she starts unravelling her story. Josie tries not to giggle until she swallows her coffee. Her hand covers her mouth, just in case Gramma says something that makes her laugh quick and hard before she swallows her coffee.

"Cheam is splitting in two. There is a big crack in the mountain, a good earthquake will finish the split, so them white boys are up there day and night trying to pin it up."

"Like you really can pin a mountain together," Gramma snorts. We all look up. Sure enough, Cheam is all lit up. You can almost hear the giant machines. I can almost see them drilling holes in her.

My mom is on her feet, "Oh dear. Look-ee here. Thish here mountain is splitting in half. Ho, heck. I got me thish here old spare safety pin left over from my kid's diaper days, let's just take it and pin it all up." The laughter pops the picture.

I'm laying in the dark again.

Sto: loh women confuse me. They can take a piece of information like Cheam Mountain is splitting in half and run straight away to laughing at the white guys trying to fix it without giving two seconds thought about the consequences if it does split. If Cheam splits the whole Fraser Valley will disappear. There are pages and pages of concern over this eight-year-old memory running around my brain. The river will back up and spill over the edge of the dam created. It will be one heck of a mess. There will be dead folks and animals everywhere. Pinning it up may not work, but something has to happen.

I don't know enough to respond to this memory. I smile a little anyway. My journey is about to begin. This little snippet has defined the direction my journey will take.

I light the candle by my bed, take one last look at an old photo of me whooping it up on an old swing in some park, my fat five year old cheeks grinning ear to ear.

"Bye, bye, Willie. Hello Lilt." I pick up some tobacco and look out at the moon. I wrap the tobacco in some cloth I keep stashed in my night table and thank the moon for giving me some starting point in finding my way as a Sto: loh man in this crazy world. Good thing too. Next week is my Becoming Man Ceremony. I do not want to be the first Sto: loh man in this family to face our nation saying, "I have no idea what I'm doing or where I'm going."

"Thanks Gramma Moon—oh and you too Raven." I am not so good at ceremony. I have heard others do the tobacco-thank-you-thing full of fine language, lots of pomp and ceremony, but I can't seem to muster that pretty talk. I believe a simple "thank you" is worth as much to our Gramma Moon as it is to my gramma here on earth, so I don't mind. My journey is about to begin.

Chapter 1

The crunch is on. Getting ready for this ceremony has reached a crisis, so, naturally we are now able to handle it. We're Natives and we all seem to do well in a crisis. In fact, we never plan anything far enough in advance to prevent it from becoming a crisis. We are all flying about, busy, hurrying, short of breath and snapping at each other and laughing by turns.

Mom's house is full of women, all five of her sewing machines are roaring. There are coloured cloth strips everywhere. Beats me how the women can remember whose strip is whose. I don't see any plans for the blankets anywhere —excuse me that would be 'patterns', not plans. I watch them from a distance for a moment. They are looking at each other yakking or laughing and grabbing strips of cloth without paying any attention to which strip they choose. Like magic, the blankets take shape.

The women are all my blood relatives, except Jenny, my Uncle Eli's wife. Lily, Josie and Anne are my mom's sisters.

I don't know much about Jenny, except she makes my uncle cluck his tongue, wink and say, "Going to be a hot time tonight," every Friday when he goes home. She whacks the middle of his back gently every time he says it, then laughs and says, "Be quiet." But on Fridays, unlike any other day, she greets him at the door with a big smile. I get it now, but it used to confuse me when I was younger and had spent the weekend with Thomas, my cousin.

The women are all in various states of the sewing-blanket-business. Callie is my sis, older by lots. Josie is cooking. I take it she doesn't sew. I don't know if she doesn't know how, but I have never seen or heard of her ever doing it. I never asked, but whenever we are getting ready for a giveaway Josie always cooks.

All my brothers before me had this ceremony and my sister had a Becoming Woman one. Hers, I remember. Josie baked a giant cake with an art piece of Callie's on it. Chocolate. "No cake for the men, too girlie," Josie says. Damn. I like Josie's cake. I can handle girlie if cake is all it is.

"Pies, pies, pies, that's man's food," she says. The pies are coming out of the oven looking better than store bought. I can smell the fillings: pumpkin Momma had canned up at Halloween, cherries carefully pitted and frozen, apples preserved as pie filling, salmonberries, blueberries, saskatoons and blackberries. The scent of the lighter fruits wafts about under the heavy scent of the more intense fruits and the pumpkin creating a medley of teasing smells. Funny, I thought I remembered Mom saying we were out of berries sometime during early spring. I wince. She hates to say we are out of anything. "Eat, eat, eat," is her biggest expression of love. It must have hurt her to hang onto these berries for this occasion.

My brothers are sitting in the living room. I call it the kids room. In a Sto: loh house the kitchen is domain of the women and the not-yet-talking kids. The living room belongs to the bigger kids; the ones who have the sense to ask for something to eat and can get themselves to the bathroom and bed on time. We are allowed to be anywhere we please, but in the kitchen the women only pay attention to the kids still wearing diapers, and to each other. In the living room the kids are in charge until bedtime. Sometimes that is not such a great idea, because we can occasionally get naughty. When the only thing that brings the women running is the sound of crying, you learn to be kind to the little ones pretty quick. You do not want three or four Sto: loh women to come charging in on you at the sound of someone crying, unless you be the one doing it. Before 8:00 p.m. the kids get to pick the TV programs. After 8:00 p.m. the men pick them until we are old enough in someone's eyes to hold our own in a grown-up conversation with the other men who, by their very size, are defined as men—according to Aunt Josie that isn't hard past six years old. If the women move from the kitchen to the living room, then we are all going to be watching *Joy Luck Club, The Colour Purple, Once Were Warriors* or some such. Today there won't likely be any women in the living room.

It's getting late, so the little guys are all sleeping or just plain out of luck about determining what's on TV, nor will they be getting any more attention from the women. 8:00 p.m. is Sto: loh for quitting time as far as the women are concerned, unless you are sick.

All the estrogen in the kitchen is overwhelming me, so I make my way down the hall to the living room. *Terminator* is on. There are four kids in my mom and dad's little family.

Mom had us all four years apart almost to the day. George is nineteen, Tony is twenty-three and Callie is twenty-seven. By September all those numbers will be even and older.

George has a stack of deer bones and an electric jigsaw next to him with a little cordless electric drill next to the saw. A grinding wheel is clamped to the coffee table. He's making bones for chokers.

Tony sits in front of a card table. On it is a tablecloth ironed completely flat. I almost chuckle. I know he had to iron it himself. Tony is kind of a big guy. Not tall, but his hands are wide and his fingers are very pudgy. The picture of him with a little iron flattening out the little cloth strikes me as funny. On the cloth are neat little piles of cut glass and brass trade beads and some of George's bones. The ones George has finished carving and drilling that is. Half the bones are sitting in a cup of tea. Bear claws, eagle and grouse claws, and bear teeth are heaped together on one corner of the table. Tony is making chokers, breastplates and armbands—likely all matching. He has a sheet of silver rolled up beside him. At the far end of the table is a roll of sinew, a leather hole punch, an engraver, and about a hundred little bars of leather with three holes punched in each one in exactly the same place. Another set of leather bars sits behind the first ones; their holes are punched out wider then the first set.

To my surprise, Sarah is seated between the guys. I pull up a chair and sit next to her. She's beading barrettes and bags and moccasin tops. In the front of the room is a trunk near full of all the stuff they have finished.

"What? No *Joy Luck Club*?" I ask Sarah. (*Terminator* gunshots ring in the background.)

"Boys can't concentrate unless someone is killing someone." George and Tony laugh. Sarah is quick and never misses an opportunity to pour water on the fire of my burgeoning male ego.

"Hey. Be nice or we'll break concentration." George replies and they laugh again.

"I would care darlin' but I ain't doing this for a woman." She slides her needle through a saucer of beads, as she speaks, not even bothering to look up at me.

"Score one for Sarah." They laugh really hard now.

Her statement overwhelms me. I realize everyone is busting their butts for me. We are gathered at my mom's house creating works of art we will barely get to see except at Pow Wows or social dances and they will be adorning someone else's back, neck, chest or wrist. As soon as something is done, into the huge trunk it goes. And my dad will be here soon. He'll take up the one last space in the corner carving spoons, forks and salad bowls in sets. He's outside now burning and adzing out the bowls. If I don't say something I will bust out crying.

"I really appreciate everything you all are doing for me," I whisper softly. Both my brothers give me the same look. I have seen this look, but rarely. It's a soft teasing far-reaching look that sets your skin to glowing. My muscles tingle and soften under the look. Sarah unfolds a TV tray, grabs a cape and a barrette and says, "Show me. Don't tell me." Sarah, I swear she must be some other brand of Sto: loh. Most of us like that mushy kind of talk—but not Sarah. Except for her occasional witty remark, she is quiet. She was quiet even when she was a baby according to Auntie Anne. This family is about as quiet as a gaggle of geese at mating time. Maybe Sarah figures we're noisy enough without her adding to it. I'm just about to ask her about her quiet, when the noise in the kitchen lulls. I know what's next; my mom just said something to the women about what us "boys aren't doing" and she is about to come flying down the hall. We all three give each other a "What?" kind of look, for just one split second, then the footsteps come and the kitchen is dead quiet, like all them women want to hear us catch what-for.

"Fire," Sarah nods at the fireplace. I jump up. I haven't actually started anything; just barely got my needle threaded so I figure I should be the one to start the fire. Mom arrives, sees me kneeling in front of the fireplace, gets a satisfied look on her face then offers us food, like that is what she came for. "When we have the fire going," qualifies the offer. We have central heating, but rarely turn it on. Previous logging has left plenty of standing dry and old stumps to be harvested in our back yard. As long as there are a couple of logs and an old sweater in this house, Momma won't turn on the furnace. "Saves hydro," she always says. I once mentioned that burning logs puts fossil fuel waste into the air and contributes to the hole in the ozone layer.

"That and hairspray, which I do not use," she retorted. She further figured it was easier for the earth to close a hole in the ozone layer than to replace water used up by the extra lakes created from damming rivers to produce hydro. "The aura of the earth is under her control, but the amount of water is finite." If you argued, you were in for a heckuva science ride through a Sto: loh woman's mind, a ride you do not want to go on—trust me.

My mom has a set of rules for us boys that she is consistent about. We eat only after we do something for her; split kindling if we are small, or if we are big enough it was logs, or folded laundry, or put away jars of jam she'd canned. After this, I will be old enough to lug the canner from the stove to the porch to cool before pulling the tray of jars out of the canner and refilling it with water to put it back on the stove.

I'm not old enough to remember if it was the same for Callie, probably not, most of my girl cousins, even the littlest not-yet-talking ones come home and pick something to do, then fly at it. The girls all seem to eat whenever they feel like it. Of course, they fix their own food. I swear, the Sto: loh men in my family would starve before they'd fix themselves something to eat. Even when we are fishing the women pack our back-packs up with food.

I remember fishing not too long ago. The packs were all loaded up. We stood them up against the nearest shade bush and just as though mom were there, none of us touched it till we'd caught the first set of fish.

I want to ask about why we are this way, but a truck pulls up. That's when I notice Sarah has a sandwich and a bowl of berries and nuts next to her. I reach over to the bowl, look at her with my best comic pitiful look, she nods, and I steal a handful of what she's got. We all look at each other.

"Focus boys," Sarah says and we chuckle. We laugh at everything. I once asked my pop how come. He held his over-size belly and said, "Keeps us buff," then he cracked up.

I look at the barrette Sarah hands me and start plotting a matching design in my head. I have been beading with Sarah since I was six. Her mom moved back to the reserve from Vancouver about that time. She came to my mom's place straight away. I remember it almost to the day. It was late summer. School was going to start soon. Wild geese were making quite a clatter in the pond. The young geese were all learning to fly. I imagined that the old ones were cheering them on. It was important for them to get in a lot of practice by late fall when they would have to leave. They needed to be good at flying to make the long trip south. I had been watching them through the window looking out onto the pond my uncle Eli had built. I heard Auntie Anne's car pulls up, but paid no attention at first, then the commotion started.

Auntie Anne was the sister next to my mom and they are pretty tight. Mom and Anne wrote letters each week to one another without fail. Now, Anne was home for good.

At first there was lots of hugging and talking and an excited kind of chatter with lots of "Look who's here!" "This is my baby." And, "This is mine," "Say hi to your Auntie Anne and cousin Sarah."

I liked the commotion because it ended with tea and cake. My mom brightened up considerably in the days following Auntie Anne's return.

I caused a near disaster not long after they came back. I was outside with Thomas all morning. They were all in the living room. We weren't used to women being in the living room. Thomas and me come flying in the door, running through the hall and into the living room to watch cartoons. We weren't looking where we were going and crashed into Sarah's tray letting fly an amazing spray of tiny coloured dots of glass. Beads clouded the air for just a second. As Thomas and I scrambled to our feet, the beads landed, bouncing all over the hardwood floor covering most of it when they settled.

Sarah stared at the space where her TV tray was; her eyes welled with tears. They never fell. I wish she had sobbed. I got this sinking feeling in my gut. I never want to see that look on a woman or a girl again.

I felt so bad I asked the floor to swallow me. It didn't, so I gathered up the beads and laid them out on her tray in a little pile. All the colours were mixed up and the beads were covered in dust, lint and hair. The pile sat there on the tray looking so wrong. I knew it was so wrong, all those beads in a dusty mixed up mess, but my six-year-old mind couldn't figure out how to straighten them out. I tried to blow the lint and dust off the beads. I wanted to die right that minute, but no one in the room was going to help me do that.

"Sorry Sarah," I slowly ventured, "What-cha-doin?"

She didn't answer. She just stared at the mess. I sucked wind.

Anne poured Sarah another round of beads. Momma disappeared for a moment and returned with two nail files and a pillowcase. She set up another TV tray, then dropped a hard sounding, "Separate them out."

She pulled a small knife from her apron pocket and showed us what she meant. It took a while to separate them all out. My mom joined us, rolling the piles of separated beads in her fingers and blowing on them just hard enough to get rid of the dust, hair, and lint without losing the beads. Auntie Anne helped her.

I want to chuckle now at the picture we all made gathered around that TV tray like it was an altar and every stroke of the nail file was a Catholic bell-ringing by Thomas and I—like you see altar boys do in church. The careful blowing of my mom and Auntie Anne was angel's breath cleaning the glass beads and our spirits. We were all getting Sarah ready to make glass prayer gardens for some other little girl or boy.

After cleaning the beads, I watched Sarah conjure flowers from them like magic. Little tiny gardens popped up. I had to try it. I knew I couldn't conjure them, but I figured I could I copy whatever she was making.

"Making a barrette," she finally answered my first question.

"What'cha goin' to make next?"

"Another one." She picked up a few beads with her needle.

"Can I try?"

"Sure." She threaded me up a needle. More than that would have interrupted her work. I watched. I have no idea why, but my pudgy little boy fingers wrapped themselves up in the work just fine. The designs Sarah conjured appeared on my cloth. We were on a roll. We teamed up over the years.

Every Saturday that it rained throughout the late fall, winter and early spring, we sat at a TV tray—each beading our little hearts out. She would begin with a single barrette and I would make the match. She would make a bag, and then I would make a cape. I watched every single girl movie there ever was made, sitting next to Sarah beading. I don't know why they call them girl flicks. I liked most of them. Intense, they were all intense. I think intensity scares guys. It scares me. The one that scared me most was *Joy Luck Club*. That movie opens the door to the secret space of motherhood. It shows what you never want to see as a man.

Chapter 2

My pop hauls himself to the wood shed every day not thirty feet from this house and I know he doesn't know anything more about Mom and her secrets than I do. He just carves. His shed has become a veritable museum over time; some of the images are characters you don't even see in most museums that pride themselves on the load of Native artifacts in them. One of my favorites is a puffin; a short squat little bird-like character with big ovoid eyes coming from his big head and beak and just four feathers in the wings falling from each side of his oversized shoulders. Some days that puffin looks comic, other days he seems to pout. Pop has him perched on top of his tool shelf unit, just below a series of masks. He's not for sale. He's Pop's personal toy.

Some of the masks were the usual eagle, wolf and raven masks that are so commercially popular, but some of them were masks Pop had taken a shine too. There is this one that looks scary, half his face is smooth, handsome, the other mean looking. The smooth side's hair is long, smooth and sleek, black human hair, the fierce side's hair is coarse, disheveled and a mix of red, brown and black horsehair. Pop carves mainly the West Coast Native commercial stuff that white people like, but now he will be carving bowls, spoons and plates etched with family crests that the women in our family like to receive as gifts.

Mom has never gone to town alone, at least not that I have heard; but then, that might be one of the secrets in her space. Food appears on our table regular and twice a year we head to the nearest town to buy clothes. No one talks about how all this happens. It dawns on me that my folks are business people; one of them must know about marketing, accounting, sales, trade and commerce. One of them must plan, organize and budget and keep track of all this. That would likely be my mom's secret. I can't picture Pop even having a secret. They must talk some about it, but I have never heard them. I watched *Joy Luck Club's* secret run-ins these gals have with various authorities and I prayed my mom never opens the door to her secret spaces.

Sarah and I sold most everything we made. Sarah's beadwork took us to every Pow Wow within 300 miles of home. Well, that and Mom and Auntie Anne's bannock stand. Mom and Auntie Anne could make bannock like nobody's business. I remember the line-ups to their giant wok and propane stove. That bannock stand and Pop's carving got us a recreation vehicle complete with an awning. Sarah and me made my Grass Dance outfit and her Fancy Dance outfit. Mom and Pop tended the table while Sarah and I danced our summers away. We hit every Pow Wow in the Northwest and finally ended up in Montana one summer.

We split the money 60/40. Sarah and I figured the design was worth 20 percent. Our moms made us put the money in the bank. The money gathered interest on top of the price we received. Here I am fifteen with several thousand dollars in the bank. Next week I will be a man, a man of means.

"Damn, Sarah. I am sure glad Thomas and me spilled your beads years ago." I hold up a near finished cape. She peeled off one of them skip-jump-raven-push kind of laughs. My brothers joined in.

"Boy. I really don't know how your mind works." Sarah has to stop beading while her shoulders shake with laughter at her own joke. The rest laugh harder.

"Thanks," I wink. She sits up straight. "Till just now I didn't know you thought it did." She whacks me then chuckles some more.

"Yeah," Tony says, "When did that start, you think?" Tony asks George. They are on a roll, my brothers.

"Come on Tony. I remember once he had a thought." George says.

"Yeah," Tony says incredulously, "What thought was that George?" He knows what thought George is talking about and I do too. I am laughing before George gets it out.

"Yeah. It was back in 1990, thought he'd paint his brand new bike." George says nearly falling off his chair.

"With house paint," Tony finishes.

I blush. "Doggone it you guys. I will be eighty-years- old and you'll still be digging up that old, 'my brilliant little brother painted his brand new bike' story for anyone who'll listen."

"We'll likely still be laughing at it too," Sarah adds.

"Whooeeeh. That was one ugly paint job." George is laughing so hard he has to stop what he's doing.

My brother Tony and sister Callie had worked caddying at the golf course all year. They saved some money and bought me a brand new Little Mighty-Mite Mustang looking mountain bike. It was blue. Thomas and me figured we would fix her up all fancy. We dug about in his basement for cans of colours. Latex house paint doesn't sit on metal too well. We didn't know that. We painted. It didn't look good going on. We figured it would dry nice, so we just carried on. It didn't. The streaks were terrible but the paint was dry. So I hid it in Thomas' basement.

Days later, Tony and Callie must have figured it out, maybe Uncle Eli saw it in the basement and told them. They asked me about my bike. I got all nervous and twitchy. I lied and told them that it was at Thomas' so we could ride around together.

"Thomas spends more time here then you do there, maybe you ought to bring it home and ride it here." Callie said.

I just couldn't hold back the tears. I was so ashamed of mucking up the bike they worked so hard to get me. I couldn't slow the picture down enough to sort through the shame, the realization of their efforts, my failure to appreciate what I had and so I just cried. Tony picked me up. We all trouped over to Thomas' house, me crying all the way. They took one look at the bike and cracked up.

"Damn, what were you thinking boy?"

This remark did shrink the complexity of the hurt to just plain embarrassment over doing such a bad job. I couldn't tell if that was helpful or not. I went from being a traitor to just being dense. Even on reflection I am not sure which was worse. They fixed up my bike. Thomas and me got to help. We learned a lot about paint while we were doing it. In my remembering I stop beading for a minute and stare off into space at all the images around it.

"Focus boys," barely leaves Sarah's lips when I hear my pop.

"Ha-ay. My beautiful wife, you're still here. I can't believe you're still here." I know what's coming next. What is it about us that makes the same ol', same ol', so satisfying to the soul?

"I can't believe it either, you old fool, get in here." And she laughs the happiest laugh you ever heard, just like it was the first time he ever said it. Pop says this like he's been gone for half of forever, and not at all like he is coming in from the shed in the front yard. The shed is where he always is when he is not in the house or on the road with Momma and the rest of us in tow. I don't remember Pop going anywhere without Mom and the lot of us. I want to be that much in love sometime, maybe I just want to be that loving.

There's a commotion outside coming from the truck that just pulled up. George and Tony make their way to the patio doors and pull the curtain back. I can see Thomas and Uncle Eli struggling with something big they are trying to take off the truck, but I can't see what it is yet. George and Tony run to help. I feel Sarah's eyes on me and go back to beading before she says, "focus." They bring in this flat big carving, must be eight by five feet. It has a door handle on it.

"What is that? Looks like a door." As soon as I see my cousin put his hands on his hips and bend at the waist, I am sorry I said that.

"Well, I am glad it looks like a door cousin, because it's handy when a door looks like a door." They all crack up. It is stunning. Laminated cedar all carved like a *chilkat* with every Clan of the West Coast etched into it.

"It's huge!" I say. Not again—how come I always seem to say the obvious? I am going to be sorry for this one too.

"Well good thing we aren't munchkins then, huh?" Uncle Eli offers with deadpan seriousness.

"Well, maybe we should have made it small, Dad." Thomas tells him like both of them must be just plain dense. "It is for munchkins you know."

"Would have saved us a peck of trouble, son," from Eli, like they were just the biggest pair of darn fools.

"Well, generally speaking the door has to fill the size of the hole it's covering, no matter what the size of the person passing through it." Thomas informs his pop in a mock condescending tone.

"Yeah," Uncle Eli responds feigning deep thoughtfulness, "that way you keep the rain out when it's closed."

"Willie wouldn't know about that," my mom adds. Pop can barely contain himself. His slightly overweight belly is shaking.

"I know, I know. I never close the door," I add. "What's it for?" I ask another dumb question. Where did I leave my mind today?

"A doorway," Sarah cannot resist. I am way too easy. Another skip-jump-raven-push laugh. She doesn't even stop beading it came so easy.

"Daycare," Tony decides to give me a break and answer my question.

"Daycare?" I can not for the life of me appreciate the break Tony just gave me.

"Is there an echo in here?" Tony takes back the break.

"You do remember going to daycare while your ma worked her pretty fingers to the bone don't you son?" Dad put his arm about my mom's waist.

"I taught *Halkomelem,* dear, to children who could not read. That is a language and you do that with your mouth not your fingers, Hon." I must be a chip off the old block cause now we are all laughing at Pop.

"Got to give something to the new one they're building." Eli finishes.

"How do you know what size to make it?" It was out, too late to take it back.

"Well. If you'd wake up in woodworking class for thirty seconds at a stretch, you would know the answer to that, little brother." George leaps on the opportunity.

"Does he sleep in class?" Mom is seriously concerned over this statement. The boys do me a favor by laughing. She figures, incorrectly, that they are kidding, waves her hand at them and laughs along. I join them, but it is more like comic relief. The interplay becomes so complex we can't figure who is laughing at what. That is funny in itself and Tony and George laugh all the harder.

"Plans?" I ask. "They have plans?" No one laughs.

The Band had been talking about pending plans for the daycare, high school and senior's complex for a year, but this is the first we heard that they actually were completed and in the hands of someone from this reserve. The government dragged the business of getting the plans finished.

There was a Longhouse attached to it. There was always something not up to code about that Longhouse that drove the architects back to the drawing board over and over again.

"Yep," Pop answers, "they have plans. 'Fact, plans is all they have."

"What do you mean?" This from Mom. No one will turn this into a laugh. Not unless they want to see how strong carving can make a man's hands over forty years. Pop doesn't like us teasing Mom.

"The plans cost so much that all they can afford is building materials, no wages." Pop is looking right at Mom as he answers. He doesn't seem the least bit upset.

"Oh no," she says.

"They have a plan to solve that problem though." He hands her a piece of paper. "They are asking every man who can hammer and saw to volunteer at least an hour before work and an hour after work to help build it. Those who can't handle a hammer and saw, will dig, cook or babysit while every man, woman and large child works. Those who aren't working at regular jobs can fly at it all day."

"Well what about feeding our families?" Mom's clearly nervous; she starts straightening things out that don't need to be straightened when she is nervous. Right now she is tugging at the mantel shelf ornaments, shoving them this way then that.

"Read on. They got plans for that too. They plan to fish and hunt, well not exactly them, but the teenagers, like young Will here will be sent into the bush and out on the river. I believe the women are meeting this Sunday. Lizzie is talking garden, berries, and roots... "

"What about the mortgages?" Mom cuts in.

"Well, our homes are paid out at twenty-five percent of our income. Twenty-five percent of nothing dearest would be nothing. Government subsidy will have to cough it up. Since they won't pay the architects over-runs created by their piecemeal demands; the Band looks to getting them to cough up in mortgage subsidies. Most of us are self-employed. Those who have regular jobs will keep on working, but the carvers, fisherman, space loggers and shake splitters will be busy framing and living off earth's bounty. Tighten up boys, it's going to be a berry-fish kind of summer."

"Whose idea was that?" Mom is staring at some glass figurine of a wolf on the mantle shelf of the fireplace like she is wondering why she ever bought it. Her voice sounds whimsical and calmer.

"Old Lizzie's," Pop replies.

No more will be said. We need to switch direction from questioning the Band to going along with Old Lizzie.

"They figure it will only take a couple months to have the building framed, wired and plumbed," Tony says wiggling the sheet and trying to find something good about going ahead with this.

"Well... " Thomas says, "we got a door."

We all crack up.

"It's a start," he carries on some more, "Next Monday better tell our new man to purchase himself a belt, hammer and saw." Then my pop says, "Well son, your first job will be building the daycare until fishing season starts. Wages are a little low but it's honourable work boy."

A million questions are running through my head. I am trying to think of who can read plans and organize the construction of a project this big. It is not just a daycare. A new high school is attached to it and they intend to attach a new senior's center to that. The Band wants the older kids and the little kids and the Elders all in one spot. Traditionally, the Elders would teach the young adults and the little ones. The teenagers would be available to help teach the little ones. They plan to pair us up and teach language to us all. The kids in between these age groups will stay at their school next door until they are teenagers. I don't know much about building. Like George said, I fall asleep in woodworking a lot, but I know there is more to this than putting a belt on and picking up a hammer and a saw. There will be landscaping too, parking lots, kitchens and a Longhouse in the middle of it all. Oh, man. I saw models and pictures of it. It isn't so easy as framing a shed.

"Does anyone in this community know how to read plans?" I ask.

"Focus," from all three of my male relatives.

"We don't need to figure nothing out till next week." Pop adds. Then it will be a crisis and that we can handle, I tell myself.

"Foods up," from Mom, ends the discussion. I saunter into the kitchen to get my food and my aunt whispers in my ear, "Now don't you go worrying yourself about all that till Monday." She knows me too well.

Outside on the back picnic table, all of us are quiet, so I know they have the same misgivings about this daycare business as I do, but I also know we don't have much in the way of choices at this point. We have to build it. Someone will have to figure out how to read blue prints and the rest of us will have to learn to take orders. Forks click on dishes and the night folds us up slow and easy like it knows we are about to have a hard time. We eat quickly. There is still a lot of work to do before Saturday.

I feel like a conundrum: a riddle no one can solve, not even myself. I like to do beadwork like the women and bar-becuing the way Sto: loh men do. No one minds what anyone does. It is just as common for women to handle hammers and saws as babies and beads, that isn't what makes me feel like a conundrum. It is that I don't like hammering or sawing. The smell of fresh cut cedar doesn't turn me on the way it does my male relatives, but I like fishing, standing on the rock ledges, swinging a dip net under cover of night and listening for the fish and game wardens just like Sto: loh men have been doing for decades. I do not want to go out and buy a belt, a hammer or a saw. I have never gone fire fighting, or whipped up a giant chainsaw to fetch standing dry, or bucked up firewood or split cedar to make shakes. I have not space logged or done much of anything else that seems to turn Sto: loh men on. I split kindling and chopped wood at our fish camps for my mom with a fair amount of hesitation and a trace of resentment. If she were anyone else I think I would have declined. Something tells me though that building this daycare is going to do something good for me. I know it is not going to make me like building, but something, something good is going to happen to me.

. . . .

The flowers shape up under my needle nice and easy. Sarah hasn't said a word for sometime. Come to think of it, everyone has been strangely quiet for some time now. A cape gets done. Sarah already has three more sets of barrettes and bags done than I have capes—I am three behind. Unless I speed it up a bit, we will not be ready; maybe tomorrow I will start sooner. My eyes are beginning to blur from fatigue.

Mom walks in, "Go on all of you, it's midnight. Gramma and the girls are coming over to quilt tomorrow. Before you go to bed get this damn couch and chair out of here and move your stuff to one side of the room. This here trunk can be set up on the stairs. Then go to bed. 6:00 a.m. is breakfast."

I know they don't have any blankets ready for quilting. That means Momma and her sisters are going to go on sewing, probably all night. Likely Callie will stay up with them. I want to go on stitching beads, but my vision is blurring anyway, so after shifting furniture, like I'm told, I turn in.

Chapter 3

Dreams are odd things. They patch life together in strange patterns. Shep, an old dog I once owned, shows up. We are hill climbing: Shep, myself and Thomas, wander around under one of those rare West Coast suns, the kind that skims the skin with just enough heat to get your mind slowed down, but not hot enough to make you uncomfortable. Must be August, because the berries are ripening. We pick a few berries; toss rocks, run, then walk. Nothing is going on in my mind and no words are exchanged between Thomas and I, then it ends.

The shopping mall is full of strange people. I clutch my mom's skirt so tight my fingers ache. We aren't anywhere near home—must be Vancouver. Sarah is holding my other hand. She is almost a head taller than I am. She looks at me, reaches in her pocket and hands me a green apple, carefully peeled and wrapped in waxed paper, then she smiles.

The Pacific National Exhibition is a cacophony of lights, colour, sound and titillating smells of cotton candy, hot dogs and what have you. I am on my first roller coaster ride. We are slowly climbing the first hill. I am praying I don't scream like a girl.

My brother whispers, "Remember, the word is Whoa-ah. That'll keep you from screaming like a girl." I thank Tony.

Just before the roar down that first hill, I start hollering "whoa-ah." It works. On the way up the second small hill I wonder why none of us tell the girls to say whoo-ah. I guess guys have secrets too, not as serious as the ones in *Joy Luck Club*; but we have secrets.

There is mud everywhere. Auntie Annie and Mom are ahead of us, digging for something called clams. The smell is unforgettable, thick almost spongy. There are some kind of green, clear plastic-like strips everywhere on the surface of the mud. I ask Momma why all the green plastic strips are there. She tells me it's seaweed not plastic. The water is warm to the touch, the mud cool. The bucket is full and we are heading back. I turn and see the water chasing us. I get a little scared and grab my mom's skirt. She and Auntie Anne laugh. I let go.

The sun is setting; its glow creates a silhouette effect on the line of gamblers sitting across from us. The scent of fresh cut grass complements our line of singers. The bones are pure white; one has a mark across its midsection. The voices singing are intense, deep, full and round. The drumbeat excites. We are bouncing. It is our turn to hide the bones. The girl across from me sits still, so still. Her face is round. Under other circumstances she would look so warm and cuddly, but now, steel is filling up her body, oozing out her eyes. She is the guesser in a serious game of *Lahal*. She relaxes in position, tosses her head of amazing hair, big hair, long hair, lots of it. The woman beside her looks arrogant.

She is slimmer, smaller, but somehow looks just like the guesser, sister, I decide. I sing harder. We play all day and into the night. We lose.

· · · ·

Morning comes too soon. Mom rattles pots and pans and hollers. I stumble into the shower and out again; my brothers are lined up for the same purpose. The smell of eggs and toast wafts up the stairs. We straggle downstairs after shaving, showering and whatever. There is a stack of unquilted blankets on the floor in the corner, six or eight of them. The women were up late.

"What time did you get to bed?" I address this question to Mom.

"Three. How many eggs you want?"

"Mo-om," I scold her.

"Hush and eat," she snaps.

Pop puts his plate in front of her. She gives him a scolding look, then loads it up. Pop keeps complaining about gaining weight, but goes right on eating like a teenager. I know it worries my mom. His brother is the same, got that sugar disease: diabetes. He could get over it if he would cut back on food, but then he says he wouldn't enjoy his life so much. The local doctor once told Uncle Eli that he was going to die if he kept on eating like that. Eli asked him how much he was paid to tell him that. The doctor told him, then Eli responded,

"Got news for you doc, I am going to die no matter how I eat."

I don't know if Pop feels the same as Eli, but he is catching up to his younger brother's size.

The women on the floor of the living room have packed up their bedding and are entering the kitchen. That means Pop and me will be eating outside. I don't remember ever being told to eat outside. I just know that that is what my pop and my brothers do when there are so many women over.

The movement through breakfast starts out slow and cumbersome then picks up speed. Sarah says we got time to do a little beading before school. We work. Half a cape, one side of a barrette and a bag, then we pack it in. As we ready ourselves to go out the door, our elder girl cousins with their babies come in. Suzie is Sarah's older sister. Jay is Lily's daughter and our cousin. One is married, the other is a single mom. Their kids are not talking yet, both are two-years-old. We give the kids a squeeze, tease the women and then we are off.

Sarah is in her last year of high school, one of the few in our family who will actually finish at the right age. Me, I'm in my second year. Sarah is doing well, an honour student. I don't do too badly in my academic subjects, but I can't deal with Woodworking or Physical Education. It is not that I am not strong or good at sports or anything. I like playing football, but that has nothing to do with Physical Education. I just can't handle those white boys who take everything way too seriously. Or maybe it's me who takes them too seriously. Tony keeps telling me not to. Every chance the jocks get, they say something crude about 'Indians' and I have no idea how many times the PE instructor has said,

"You're not on the reserve boy, push," or the jocks have asked me about getting my wick dipped. When I hear Tony telling me to not take them so seriously, I hear "put up with it" in my mind.

"How did you manage it, Sarah? Twelve years of these people."

"Oh, I don't take them too seriously, Bud." Bud's my nickname when we are alone.

"Oh yeah, put up with them," I say out loud.

"Not really, just don't believe them. I don't believe for a moment they have thought for one split second about what they are talking about. Ever!"

"What do you mean?"

"Racists are thoughtless is all. They don't think, not one of them, least not many I go to school with."

"How can you not think?"

"How can you be racist and thoughtful?" Sarah replied and I laughed at that.

So she means don't take them too seriously is actually about them, not about me. That makes it easier. I play with that. If they were thoughtful, they would have better words coming out of their mouth. I know they don't treat each other very well. They rag on their buddies for losing a game, being late, and not being where they are supposed to be. Just about anything gets their goat.

"They have the emotional maturity of a tantrum throwing wounded wolf pup," Sarah continues, "would be downright unfair to treat them seriously." We both laugh now.

"Do they say ugly things to you?" I ask.

"Yeah," she answers flatly, "but that just makes it easier to ignore them—you know what I mean?"

I shrug my shoulders. "I think so. I am not sure, but I think so."

"What you need to do is make friends with the ones they don't want. They are usually the thoughtful ones. Then you find out that the noisy ones are the only pains in the butt and they are generally in the minority. Because they are so noisy they are the only ones we see, but when you start paying attention to the others, the noisy ones kind of disappear."

"Yeah... but who wants to hang with a nerd?"

With an ironic tone Sarah replies, "How thoughtful is that?"

I stop talking about it. I know someplace inside she is right, but I haven't had a chance to whirl around it and so I can't see it just now. Best to let it sit. Sarah opens a page and draws a hangman's noose, challenging me.

"All right!" and I roll up my sleeves.
She hangs me just as the bus pulls up to the school.

It is lunchtime. I sit next to Paul, one of the nerds in the cafeteria. He looks just a little confused, then slides over to give me more room to sit.

"How is it going?" he asks politely trying not to sound suspicious. I answer honestly. "I am dead dog-tired from last night. I have been getting ready for my Becoming Man Ceremony instead of sleeping."

He is curious about it, asks what it is, and I spend ten minutes trying to explain a thousand years of custom. He listens. A couple more guys join us. I recognize them, Joseph and Wit. There is only one high school in this town and it isn't that big, most of us know each other by name even though we may not hang out together. Paul and Wit and Joseph pretty much make up the geek clique. Pretty soon we get into a discussion about initiation ceremonies generally and how white people have lost theirs.

"Well, not completely," Paul quips, "there are still some of us pounding our chests and bellowing, even as we speak." He alludes to half the football team in the corner, belching loudly and hee-hawing about it. We laugh. They don't notice us. The conversation gets interesting.

"So, what inspired you to sit with the nerds?" Joseph asks. I almost suck wind. Tell the truth, I tell myself.

"My cousin says you are thoughtful. I think her exact words were, nerds are thoughtful, for white people that is." They crack up.

"We must seem a little crude in our disrespect," Joseph answers.

"She pointed out that I am only looking at the noisiest bunch and that blinds me to you, the thoughtful bunch."

"So did you ask her, who wants to sit with a bunch of nerds?"

"Yeah."

"What did she say?"

"How thoughtful is that?" I said hanging my head. Joseph laughed again.

"Technically, we aren't nerds," Wit says. "We hang out with Joseph, who truly is a nerd." We all laugh then.

"However, I will go with the thoughtful bit," he finishes. I look up from the laughter. Something pulls my face to the window. A doe is standing there looking in. Behind her the rest of the football team is circling in on her, getting ready to throw a bunch of rocks they are holding. I jump up but Paul pulls at my jacket. I warn him not to stop me. They sigh. I holler the biggest "NO!" I can. The doe leaps. They attempt to throw their rocks in a hurry, so most of them miss and those that strike are weakened by a poor wind-up into the throw.

The doe isn't seriously injured, but I am going to be. She got away because of my warning and the meat heads are angry. I am not going to back down but I am sure as heck not going to take on the whole football team.

"Well. We are, boys, in a bit of fix, would you say?" Wit remarks

"You think?" comes from Paul.

"I will handle it," I say calmly.

"Or we shall all be handled," from Wit.

"For sure," Joseph says "and I am bone weary of being handled, but am not sure digging in is the best solution."

"On the other hand, stubbornness may work. For sure we can't use intelligence." Wit is funny.

"What's up Chief?" I look behind me, beside me, all around me.

"Hey... we're talking to you."

"Well, I don't believe he is old enough to be a Chief," Wit answers.

"You don't have to answer for me Wit, my friend, I am pretty good at getting my own self into trouble." My table laughs, the football players don't.

I lean forward, "I thought you boys were sporty, so I

gave the doe a fair chance. I know you wouldn't want to play football with a bunch of cripples. It ain't manly enough for you."

This shallow appeal to their sense of manhood works. There is a lovely tense moment. One word could change my history at this school. The line separating the players from me is invisible but omnipresent in my mind. No one moves. We just stare at each other.

The lead football player says, "Well don't do it again." He leaves with his followers in tow.

"I would not have guessed that. I would have thought playing cripples would be their idea of the ideal in sportiness," Wit says. We hiss out a quiet snicker.

Paul changes the subject to geometry. I believe I can make it through this. My cousin Thomas has arrived. He stands there staring at me with his tray in his hands for a split second. He's got this "What?" kind of look on his face as he gives each one of the nerds a look. I shrug. He shrugs, then sits.

About halfway through the conversation I notice Wit has a limp-wrist. He is pretty in a girl kind of way. Clean slender high-arched eyebrows and slim. The others don't seem to notice it. I wonder... nah. I watch Thomas stare at Wit's hand gestures. He sees it too. *Please Thomas, don't say anything. I am having some fun with white boys for the first time in ten years of having to share the same air space with them.* Thomas looks right at me, catches my "don't say it" look and says nothing.

On the bus home Thomas sits next to me.

"So, what about Wit?" he asks.

"You think he's gay too?" I ask

"Yup."

"Does it bother you?"

"Somewhat."

"What do you want to do?"

"Absolutely nothing. In fact, I am not sure why we were bothering to eat with them today. So I don't have any clue, cousin. You sat with them, I presume you have some reason for this, so the ball is in your court."

"I am not sure either. But it felt good, in some strange way. Like for the first time, I was really at school."

"More connected?" he asks.

"Yeah." I surrender to this new sense of finally belonging.

"I think we ought to talk to him though," Thomas adds.

"Why? What will we say?"

"I don't know. Maybe just let him know it's okay, but we aren't like that. I don't want to break anyone's heart; man, woman or beast."

"Maybe," I answer.

"Think about it anyway," Thomas cautions.

"Maybe we should just let it go. Maybe he isn't attracted to us. Maybe he just finds us interesting." I can hear myself making excuses and even I can't stand the words dropping out of my mouth. Thomas cuts me off.

"Maybe if cows could fly we would spend our lives ducking cow pie."

Chapter 4

The living room is alive with women stitching flowers, dia-
monds, crescent moons and columns onto blankets. Plain
ribbon-shirt looking quilts become works of art. They are
chatting and laughing, hardly looking at what they are doing.
School seems a million miles away. I sit next to Sarah. We
don't have near the space anymore. We have to sidle along
the wall to escape stepping on the blankets, needles and the
women quilting. No one seems to notice us.

"Thanks," I begin saying to Sarah.

"If you think you are going to kill some time by getting
all mushy for five minutes think again," she says and hands
me a threaded needle. I begin schlepping through the cloth
and laying the first bead, still staring at her pattern, it's a
new one. This one looks special—more colour than usual.

"No. I made some new friends is all."

"Oh yeah, surprise, surprise." I told her what happened,
careful not to stop working while I talked. She was quiet for
a moment after I spoke.

"Don't think they will stick up for you cousin."

"What? You think they would betray me?"

"Nooo," she lets go slowly, "I don't think they would
consider it betrayal."

I have to think about that one.

"We are Clan-based, they are 'people' based—democracy is about 'people' in general, not Clan in particular."

It slides out easy. I don't get it. It sounds simple, but I don't understand what she could possibly be talking about. She sounds like she knows something though, so I ask her what she means by all that. This time, my older brothers lean into our conversation. She picks up the volume so they can hear over the din of the others in the room. She says a whole lot about, "elections, universal freedom, individualism... " that makes no sense to me. Human rights versus family and Clan obligations I understand. We don't have rights in this family. The kids are permanently grounded. We don't go anywhere the family doesn't go. We busy ourselves with whatever the family is busy at and everyone, grammas, grandpas, uncles, aunts, nieces, nephews, grandkids, everyone, belongs to every house we set our feet in. We are ruled by maxims, beliefs everyone calls them, maxims is what they are:

'We don't watch people work.' This means if you see someone doing something you jump in and help them out. 'Women eat anytime. Men eat after their chores are done.' Their chores are defined by what the head women need done. 'The head woman is always someone's mother.' She is not elected, nor is she self-appointed. She seems to be recognized by her siblings and the men around her the way my mom is recognized and it seems to have something to do with her knowledge. It is a slippery kind of recognition. If my mom doesn't know anything about something she hands over the reins to some woman she knows does know about whatever. Everyone switches allegiance to this other woman. It is never said out loud in any direct kind of way. She will just casually ask Ellie what she thinks and like magic we all know—Ellie be the boss here. No votes, no election, no platform, just simple acknowledgement.

"Give me some kind of example." I need more.

"Well, thirty years ago, there was a war the Vietnam War. Some of the guys around here volunteered for the Korean War, so your dad's favorite young cousin talked about volunteering for the Vietnam War—Gramma nearly threw a fit. She asked Eli who he fought in Korea and he told her:

"'People who looked just like us,' Then she asked him,

"'Who won?' and he answered,

"'White people.'

"Pop wanted to build a family with your mom and he talked his favorite little cousin into falling in line with his prospective Gramma's point of view. Nothing more was said. Pop's cousin dared not go. No one in this family was keen on repeating the Korean experience; so his cousins going to Vietnam would not have been a good way to start for Pop. Now white people would put that question to a vote. There would be a campaign around it, a vote would be taken and if the vote was won; they would go to war. They would then start drafting men. Your dad's cousin would not have gone, even if that happened Gramma said no, well not exactly no, but she made her feelings known. No man in the history of this family has betrayed the heart of its women. That is not democratic, it's Clan."

I got it. That was plain as plain could be. What other people think is kind of irrelevant to us. The whole Clan moves as a unit, and the feelings of its women are the center of its unit. Us kids are all spokes in the family wheel, the women stand at the hub and the men wrap themselves around those spokes to make sure the wheel turns around free and easy.

"Like having this Ceremony?" I ask, testing to see that I have it right.

"Like having this Ceremony and working it the way we do," she affirms.

"What do you mean?" I don't get the working it the way we do part.

"We don't give away store bought goods to invited guests," she says, holding up the beadwork she is working on.

"Others do?" I ask, surprised.

"Yeah," she says.

"That would be simpler," I offer.

"Yuppers," she says.

"But not at all like my mother, who is about the most unsimple woman in the world," I finish for Sarah and resign myself to my mother's ways.

"That too," Sarah adds.

The conversation ends. There is no more to be said. Five more days to go. Tonight I have beaded daydream words into these capes. Words I want to say five nights from now. Words about discovery, about wondering, about the earth, about being Sto: loh. "I want to discover this Island, not just the Sto: loh land I know, but the whole Island." With every phrase I utter, images come up.

. . . .

Pictures of the Rockies loom up, ribbons of highway winding through them and little bodies of men, pushing horse carts up the mud, in the rain, in the snow, all of them laying out the first highway. Many of them are Tsimpsians, who come all the way from Prince Rupert, a thousand miles away, to build these roads. Navvy Jack, our distant relative popped into the picture along with these tall, squarely built Northern Salish people. The Tsimpsians are bigger, they are stronger, and they work harder and longer. They are grimmer looking than my folks on first sight, but they all have that same skip-jump-raven-push kind of laugh that every Salish person I know has. Some of them stay behind. They help some of us gain some height, not a lot, but some. I picture them heaving them horse carts through canyons, before blasting became a common practice.

I wonder about the loneliness of being without family. Most among them who work the roads, the railroads, or even the timber, never stay long; three months at a stretch and they go home again. I guess they figure the job would still be there when they got restless or ran out of money for trade goods or maybe they think there would be more roads.

Grandpa says white men were arriving by the shipload in those days. They still are, you just don't see it anymore. Maybe we just don't look at it or recognize it. No fanfare around new arrivals, not any docking areas or holding tanks anymore. Everything nowadays is polite and subtle, carefully obscure.

The landscape sharpens. An old Clydesdale sweats at the tether end of a cart. Four men heave and push the back end of the cart. A small man in front is pulling a rope that is wound around a bark-stripped tree. The incline seems impossible to surmount. Rain pummels the horse, cart, crew and burgeoning road. Mud shapes under the feet of the men and the wheels of the cart sink down into it. It becomes inches deep. Sliding, slipping and pulling they struggle with the elements and the business of road building. The man in front pulls at the rope and sings. Some white guy in front is hollering, "Don't you kill that sonofabitchin' horse now."

A small Asian-looking guy drops ash under each wheel every time it moves even slightly. With help from the ashes the wheels grab, the men heave again, the horse moves a tad, more ash, the wheels grab again, the men heave, the horse moves; inch by inch they make their way to the top of the incline. Buckets of sweat are pouring off the whole lot.

They are each speaking in their own language at the same time; the white guy speaks English, the Asian speaks Chinese and the two sets of Indians speak Sto: loh and Tsimpsians respectively, even the horse is whinnying in his language. When they get to the top of the hill the relief is palpable. The men point their faces to the sky; let the rain wash their faces and drink some of it. The Asian skips down the hill and returns with a bucket of water, the price to pay for the privilege of doing the lightest job I guess or maybe he is just the nicest guy among them. I wonder what drove the Tsimpsians to come a thousand miles for a job like this. Rumor has it they walked all the way on old Indian trails.

Great Grandpa is there. I recognize him by the way he squats on his haunches. It is the same way my grandpa (his son), squats. His hair shines silver in the moonlight. He must be forty or more; about the same age Pop was when I first began to remember him. Does Pop look like him or am I superimposing Pop's face on Great Grandpa's. No. There is something different about Great Grandpa. One eye is much smaller than the other is. It looks like it is permanently squinting. Callie must get her one small squinty eye from Great Grandpa.

"Heckuva walk here for this, eh-boys ?" the white guy, Jimmy, says. The Tsimpsians all laugh.

"Hyeh," they say.

"You sticking the winter out, Lapogee?"

"Nah" he says softly.

"How come? Why, you could save enough money to build your squaw a mansion."

Lapogee loathes the sound of Jimmy's language, particularly when he says squaw, but he does not complain or challenge Jimmy.

"Somebody might rob me," Lapogee offers instead.

"Put it in the bank," Jimmy says it like this Indian must be a little thick.

"Which earth do you live on, Jimmy? They don't let Indians put money in a bank." The guys laugh. The whole crew, even Charlie, the Chinese guy, laughs.

"They don't let Chinese put money in the bank either," he quips and slaps his knee like this is just too funny.

"How come? Your money is as good as mine?"

"We are children in the eyes of the law, Jimmy. We are big enough to work, but not grown up enough, in the eyes of your law, to be men." They fell quiet. Jimmy shook his head, didn't even do his customary, "Oh."

The rain kept coming. Jimmy stood straighter. Tomorrow was going to be another deadly day. On days like this, they generally lose a man or two.

"I don't suppose this does much good for you all, but I respect youse. I respect that you don't hate us. I respect that you all know how to work and git along. I respect youse and how you don't get tired of what the government's doing. Cause I get so tired when I hear it." With that he removes his hat and turns in.

They are all light years away from this thing called government and each and every one of them knows it. I can feel my great grandpa not understanding how one white man doesn't know what the other one is doing; not understanding how disconnected they are, but I can feel him accepting Jimmy's respect.

• • • •

The picture disappears from my field of vision, in its place is my cousin's garden shining up at me from a woman's cape. It is more meticulous than usual—more uniform and shinier.

47

One cape. One memory. One discovery. I hope my life journey is as easy as beading a garden. I am staring at the next garden. The barrette is a rose, just one big rose. It doesn't look like a wild one. It looks like the kind my Momma grows in her trellis in the front yard, blood red and sweet smelling. Sarah's using three colours of red to make it. The leaves are so detailed and the flower so real, I want to get a scissors and clip it from the imaginary vine it is attached to. I image up Momma's trellis and begin a new garden—a rose garden, blood red and beautiful.

• • • •

Jimmy is sitting on a log piece musing over a steaming cup of coffee. Great Grandpa is looking out onto the land that heads homeward.

"How the Sam hell we gonna get that mud to be a road with the little bit of gravel we got here?" Jimmy says this out loud.

"Slide that mountain down into the valley below. Peel the mud back. Cord them logs we are cutting, chink the logs with mud, then lay the gravel. If we are quick we can tar it," someone offers.

"Road won't last," Jimmy argues.

"Will if we cake enough mud overtop the cord wood," Grandpa adds.

"You think it will stick?" Jimmy is now seeing a plan shape up and wondering if it just might work.

"Should, it's half clay that's why it's so slippery, should work like glue."

"What we going to peel it back with. It's a mountain, Lapogee."

"We must fashion some kind of big plough maybe," from Charlie, "like a cowcatcher."

"Maybe... maybe that might work."

The sun comes up from behind. None of these men have seen her rise for weeks. The sun's light just seems to magically appear. They seen it set every day, but they haven't seen it rise.

"No Sunrise Ceremony from the back of a mountain," Gramma always said. Now I can see why. I am almost getting the feeling about what she must have been driving at, when Jimmy takes a turn in the conversation.

"You speak pretty good English there, Lapogee."

"I speak pretty good *Halkomelem* too," he says and swallows his coffee chuckling.

"I bet you do. Do you read at all?"

"No," Great Grandpa stares at the ground for a bit, then adds, "you?"

"Well not as well as I would like. My English ain't as pretty as yours."

"You teach me to write. I'll teach you to speak," Grandpa offers.

"Yeah?" He is unable to contain his excitement.

"Yes," Great Grandpa corrects him.

"Yeah?" Jimmy doesn't get it.

"No. Yes."

"Yes?"

"Yes," they click cups and laugh.

The road crew fashions a plough share from a cedar tree like the cowcatcher in front of trains. Jimmy isn't sure it will last very long. They bend some tin over the adzed front edge. They angle it into the mountain, then they all push while the horses try to drag. They work like mad scraping the mud off the mountain into the valley below. When the plough breaks, they fashion another one. Two of the men cut trees and skin them, then pile the logs in readiness for the end of the road making.

Great Grandpa is right. The valley rises and the mountain shrinks and the road smoothes itself out just enough for a horse and buggy to get up and down the hill. The more they scrape off the easier the work. They take two feet off that mountain on both sides, and build the little valley up almost eight feet. The incline changes. The rain stops about mid-day and the mud starts to dry hard like stone in places where it is thin. They lay logs, mud and gravel in a hurry on the bottom slopes trying to level the road out a little more. They tar her next morning. All during the peeling, laying and tarring, Jimmy and Lapogee talk about words, and the alphabet. Lapogee keeps correcting Jimmy. Jimmy keeps wanting to know why this and why that. Grandpa does not know the why, just the how and keeps having to say, "because it is proper."

Great Grandpa comes to the conclusion that Jimmy was a very large three-year-old and says so in Tsimpsians then *Halkomelem* to the others. Oddly enough the Asian guy understands and laughs along with them. That makes them laugh all the harder.

"How the heck did he learn the language? He must be good at listening," one of the big Tsimpsians says in his language and tugs at his ears.

"I listen. I watch. I learn," he says.

"What's your name?"

"Charlie," he answers.

"That's not Chinese," they say.

"It is now," he answers. They laugh.

By the end of the week, the road is laid, gravelled and tarred, Grandpa can read and write—print really, and Jimmy has cleaned up a considerable amount of his English. The men are beginning to understand one another. Charlie can understand all three languages, but speaks only English and that very sparingly. He tells them that he might forget Chinese if he speaks too much English. This causes some worry among the Indians. They decide not to talk so much; rather than not use the language, they just use it less. Jimmy thinks they are all nuts.

• • • •

I finish my cape just about then.

Chapter 5

"Another memory. Another garden. Roses for my Salish rose, whomever she might be." My cousin and my brothers are looking at me. Obviously, I said that out loud. I decide not to join them in the laugh that is coming. It doesn't happen. They just look at my cape.

"You're getting pretty good at that, cousin," Sarah pushes the words out gentle; careful not to let them travel too far.

All of us are looking at the garden of roses on the cape. I am seeing it like someone else did it. Two full roses on each lapel area of the cape jump up at you, trailing from them are leaves; different greens make them look three-dimensional. The vines are double strands of reddish brown beads. In the foreground, stem trailing from the main rose, there are tiny red seed beads making up the thorns—seven thorns. The leaves are layered looking, like the lighter ones are in the foreground and the darker ones are behind them. Little buds peek out between the leaves —seven buds. The roses are three-dimensional, ranging in colour from bright deep fuchsia to dark blood red. The background is a pure white and soft yellow fan-shaped shell. The shell's fan lines are pearl and the shell is flat white.

"I can't believe I just did that," some piece of me wants to weep.

"There's a lot of something in that work, boy," Tony whispers, like speaking out loud would somehow defame the piece.

"Love," George says simply. You could hear a pin drop after that for about ten long seconds. I don't believe I have ever heard the three of us talk in quite this way before. Simultaneously, we look up and at each other. We all know it's Momma's garden.

"You better decide who gets this one," Sarah says shaking her head slowly back and forth.

• • • •

The road is coming through Hell's Gate as I move onto the next cape. It is a dangerous road, but it is a road. She holds, even after the carts try her. They are behind schedule. Great Grandpa writes his first letter to his wife on the short workday—Sunday. He misses her. He doesn't say much else. I see him with that clean white paper, praying over it...well not the kind of praying white folks do when they kneel. He is just talking soft and sweet to it, like it is an old friend, asking it to be good to him, offering it his best thoughts, thanking it for laying down its life and promising not to waste it. Then he writes. The letters look uneasy on the page, like they are hesitating to land just there. They stand up just barely, but the message is clear.

"It is painful to be without you, my lovely wife, but otherwise I am doing alright. Jimmy, the foreman taught me about letters and so I feel a little closer to you by scribbling this note. I hope to see you soon. Excuse the lack of tidiness, hope you recognize the words, Lapogee."

Great Grandma can read. She had gone to the mission school at Yale. Great Grandpa had not. She is surprised to get this letter. When she reads it she thinks the "miss you, hope to see you soon" means she should come. She digs around in the closet for a pair of her younger brother's coveralls, binds her chest, dons a scarf the way she sees men do, ties up her hair, packs her bags, saddles her horse and heads for the Canyon. Just about then, Jimmy asks Great Grandpa if he knows any steady extra men who can help. They are behind schedule.

"How many?"

"A dozen or so."

"Yes, just ahead at Spuzzum."

He sends Great Grandpa on ahead to recruit some more men. Great Grandpa comes back with ten men and apologizes to the foreman.

"That's okay, two just pulled in from your village."

There is his wife, dressed like a man, winking warning at him. Standing with her is her brother who just shrugs helplessly. They work on that road together, the three of them. The pace picks up with the additional people and they pull into Revelstoke on time to meet the crew coming west. Great Grandpa makes enough money to buy land in Sto: loh territory. He buys it outside the reservation boundaries, but somehow it achieves reserve status.

I watch this tiny woman in my memory garden swinging an axe, raking gravel, and rolling tar all day for sometimes twelve hours, and I wonder where she gets the strength. She never says a word to anyone but Great Grandpa the whole time. Great Grandpa just tells folks that fella doesn't speak English. Jimmy believes him, Charlie too, especially since her brother and half the Spuzzum boys don't speak English either. The Tsimpsians don't believe him, but they kept quiet. She isn't any smaller than the Asian and with that scarf over her face like the other men; she looks liked any faceless Indian—funny how eyebrows and forehead define a face.

My Grandpa is conceived not far from Revelstoke. She conceived another child earlier, but the hard work took that baby from her before it had a chance to touch her heart. The child in Revelstoke makes it and so begins my lineage in the modern world of roads.

This garden has a half moon shaped sky colour all across the shoulder with trails of daisies and purple columbines swaying beneath it. It is hopeful, sweet and delicate. At the same time, the flowers looked insistent on just being—like Great Gramma.

"Why I believe, that is your first independent design," Sarah says.

"What?" I can't believe I have taken my moon-skirt journey in broad daylight in front of everyone and turned out a cape for which there was no matching barrette or bag.

Sarah laughs out loud, "Did you think you were following some pattern I contrived? Where were you, boy?"

I look at her barrette and blush. Hers is pink wild roses, not a bit like the one I just did.

"Where did I get this?"

I am about to get another dumb question award. My brothers laugh. They are not feeling quite so sentimental as before.

"Well, son. I believe it must be from your imagination," Tony answers and they all howl.

"It didn't come from mine. And it don't look a bit like the one that came from Sarah's," George jumps into the fracas as soon as the laughter dies, setting fire to another round.

"It's okay," Sarah assures me, "I can copy you, but we will be needing a cape to match this one." She holds up the barrette she has finished.

I look at them all and decide I better commit to the work at hand. I can't just go making up stuff right now. Sarah gets busy making barrettes and bags for the design I just did and I get started on the cape I was supposed to do. Every now and then like a mad hatter I take to chuckling about what I had done. They all giggle lightly along with me. We are tired little puppies. No more gardens of memories today.

Chapter 6

Thomas catches me in the hall.

"We gonna eat with the nerds again?"

"Hey, maybe we shouldn't call them that," I bang my locker door shut.

"They call themselves that." He is defensive.

"I don't know about you, but I am not governed by them or their language. These people, even the best of them are reasonably disrespectful if you haven't noticed, even of themselves. We have language. It's different for us."

"Okay, easy cousin, easy. You know what I'm talking about. Don't kill anymore time over it." Thomas pauses. "We need to talk about Wit."

"I know. Let's just be plain to him at lunch," I tell him.

"I have no idea how to be plain about it. So you start'er up and I'll fall in line," Thomas promises.

At lunch we are just a little too serious looking even for this group, who is generally a serious bunch. They look at us through half-closed bewildered eyes. They stare at each other for a moment, then down at their food. No one says anything for a while.

"What's up?" Wit starts.

"I am not sure how to ask this without sounding like some nosey creep, Wit."

"I don't know much about your people, pal. I do know some old guy from your village once told me, that if folks want you to know something, then they offer to tell you of their own accord. If they don't offer, then they don't want you to know. So there is no way to ask something personal without being a nosy creep. If you wrap it in sweet language you won't sound like one, but it won't change what you are." Wit's fork and knife are standing straight up. He does not want me to say anything about his limp wrists.

"Well, that about settles that. I think I just lost my curiosity." We half laugh. Wit, is funny in an intellectual way. The others just think he is being unusually intellectually funny. Thomas and I know different. We laugh with the others, but we keep our mouths shut. I steer the conversation in the direction of environmental science. They tell me about a Masters Degree Program in environmental science that is taught in some university far away. Vancouver, they tell me. I am determined to go there some day.

In class that afternoon Miss Goody Two-shoes, the instructor, lets the class know that *I* will be absent this Friday, due to a ceremony. Her voice is full of the isn't-that-so-sweet sound that particular teacher makes as she talks.

"A very important ceremony," she says, like she knows something no one else does. I have no idea why all my nice teachers do this, but when they are talking about us they emphasize syllables that don't have any emphasis in the English language. If you could write it phonetically it would be like this, "*Ay va*yree im*por*tant cayra*monee*."

Then she adds, "Would you like to tell the class about it, Will?"

"No," I answer as gently and firmly as I can.

Half the girls suck wind and hold. The guys try not to laugh. The teacher looks like a scared rabbit caught in my crossfire. She is not used to asking for something from a student and being told she couldn't have it.

"Oh... oh," then, "could we please turn to page thirty-seven of your textbooks?" She tries to recover by hiding in the textbooks. She doesn't ask me anything after that, but every now and then she glances at me with that scared rabbit look. After class, she asks me to stay behind. "If I do ma'am, I will miss my bus."

Another "Oh," and I swing out the door.

On my way out of the school, Wit catches up to me. I feel him coming up behind. I slow down.

"Say Will, you look mighty tired." His small talk prefacing what he really wants to say.

"Yeah, been to bed late and up early for three days now. I am feeling it, buddy."

"Yes. I am gay. And no. No one but you and Thomas seems to have guessed. And no, I am not likely to mistake either of you as a prospective lover. Does that satisfy your curious mind?"

"Yep. That about does it. I take it from your run through our Elder's little speech, which by the way you rapped off almost word for word. Pretty good for a white boy, that you don't want to share that with the others. Secondly, you seem to actually understand what he meant—excellent..."

"... for a white boy," Wit finishes.

"For any kind of boy," I correct him.

"Why thank you," and he bows, mocking me.

"I take it you wish this piece of information to remain, what do they say these days, confidential?" I ask gently.

"It would make my life less tiresome. If you ever want to have a conversation about it, I wouldn't be opposed to it. I am not sure I can be so open with Thomas. I mean you sat with us of your own accord. Thomas, I believe, joined you. By the way, pretty brassy response to Miss Priss," he laughs a little.

"It isn't that. I wasn't trying to be brassy. And it isn't that I don't want to tell her about the ceremony. I just didn't want to be put on display." I don't want him getting the idea I was being a scalawag.

"Ditto."

This surprises me. I don't really get the connection. I didn't think the analogy or parallel, or whatever he thought linked the two together/were the same. But then, I don't know anything about being gay in a world that really doesn't like people like him. I do know about being Indian in a world that doesn't really like people like me. The less they know about you, the less ammunition they have to hurt you—maybe that is what Wit meant. We have now reached the cafeteria doors. Wit stops, so I do too. He draws off to the side, so no one can hear us.

"Does my being gay bother you?"

"Do I mind you being gay? No. Does it bother me? Yes. I don't have a clue how to explain the difference between the two, but I have thought about it twice a day since I noticed it. Thomas and me have talked about it twice, which is a lot for us. Since I have spent some time on it and it has only been three days since I actually sat down and really met you, that tells me I must be bothered a great deal by it. I like you, so it isn't about your personality, so it must be your sexuality, your gayness or whatever you call it, that bothers me. I just haven't got a clue what is bothersome about it."

Wit cracked up. "I don't believe I have ever met anyone who stewed over this quite so deeply. Are you just into stewing over things, or is it important to your integrity to figure it out."

"I generally am a Mr. Dumb Question award-winning kind of guy who doesn't stew over much of anything, so I have no idea why I am stewing over you. Well, maybe I do know. I suppose I believe I have found a friend from the other side of the river. My friend, though, is gay. A huge number of my people are Catholics, or Catholic schooled that makes them pretty narrow-minded about 'gayness.' Gayness, that is the dumbest word I ever made up. What do you call it anyway?"

"Homosexuality."

"That sounds more like it, homosexuality, although it does not roll off the tongue so easy. I mean my folks are not the kind of people that go about gay bashing or anything like that, but there is a long hallway between gay bashing and acceptance. Being your friend could definitely be a liability. My cousin Sarah assured me that none of you would have held your ground that first day we met. But if someone were to challenge my friendship with you, I would have to hold my ground. It's a Sto: loh thing."

"Your culture demands it, mine does not, being the assumption here," he said gently careful not to disturb the air around us.

"Something like that," I answer.

"What you're saying is we don't have the same kind of marbles to put in our joint basket and you are wondering if my friendship would be worth the agony of not being able to count on it."

"Something like that," though I wasn't really sure.

"I would not have stood my ground." Wit said it from some deep place. There was a yearning in the voice. I could hear it like maybe he wanted to be able to stand his ground.

Louie, the Speaker of the Smoke House, who addressed the small group of guys that were going to go through their ceremonies this winter, called this time in our lives our "days of decision." He had said the number of decisions would rack up. We would have to make life long decisions about direction, about belief, about attitudes and about conduct. We would have to make them alone, in the dark, in our imagined selves. We would have to learn to live with those decisions. Some of our relatives would agree with what we decided, others would disagree, some might cause us pain, but we are instructed to make decisions freely, carefully, considerately and hold our ground. I wasn't sure, but I don't think Wit's last words made a difference to me. I would have to make this decision alone and hold my ground. The decisions are racking up, just like he said. Who to give the rose garden too, what to do about school, about being a Sto:

loh man and now about Wit, who comes wrapped in that package called homosexuality. I am beginning to feel too young to be doing this alone.

"The bus left." Thomas is still standing at the stop waiting for me. Wit looks like someone just slapped him with the meaning of friendship and holding your ground. Thomas did not get on the bus without me. The value of me just went up a point or two. Wit looks at me. I can see the shame on his face. For just one moment he feels honestly unworthy, not because he is different, but because he can't be the same as someone else.

"Why don't I drive you?"

This is something in our area white folks can do, when they can't offer some integrity, some loyalty, they can always get you home. I take it. I tell Thomas in *Halkomelem* that we had the talk. He nods and we swing into Wit's car.

"How did you swing a licence in tenth grade?" Thomas asks as soon as we are in the car and he settles in the backseat.

"Well, my birthday is in January, so I am sixteen. I got my licence right away. My folks gave me a car. They promised it to me if I maintained an A average."

"Cool," Thomas says and relaxes.

"You will have to direct me. I have no idea where you live?"

I direct him to the reserve. It is out of town by lots.

This town does not have a road driving straight out of it. In order to get to the road leading to my Rez, you need to wind your way past five corners, to the left and again to the right. One last left turn takes you to the road home.

Cottonwoods line the country roads here, just the same as they do the farms. Keeps the wind from blowing the dirt away between ploughing and when the corn seeds sprout. My Rez is at the base of Mt. Cheam, between the river and a slough, right where the dyke ends. We live on the flood plain across the tracks so there aren't too many houses near us, just Old Lizzie's house across the street.

"Nice house," Wit says as we pull up. We actually have a driveway—paved—a picket fence and a few rock gardens, and of course in the middle of the yard is my mom's rose trellis. Clouds are rolling in, looks like storm is coming.

I have no idea why I do this, but I invite him in. Test I guess. See how the family takes him. The older brothers are sure to catch on. Thomas says as much in our language. I look at him. He shrugs. Thomas doesn't much care what anyone's attitudes amount to. He doesn't like humans all that much anyhow. He prefers fish, deer, trees and grass; humans place a distant last, somewhere after, dogs, cats and other kinds of pets. So he is not at all worried about what everyone is going to think about us trucking around with some gay guy. I, however, am going to feel the impact of whatever attitude shows up in the mix.

"Sure, if your family doesn't mind."

"Our family welcomes visitors, but I don't know if they'll mind you," Thomas says, "you know what I'm talking about."

Wit sighs, shrugs and goes in.

"Might as well find out," I say as I swing toward the house from the car.

Sarah notices it first. She hauls me off to a corner of

the house. "Are you out of your mind, Will? You must be. I know you aren't like him, so why are you bringing him here. Shock value?"

"Sarah. He is my friend. One of the nerds you told me to talk to."

"Jeezuss. Buster is coming."

"Buster, Christ. Like I care."

"Knock it off, Will. He is a respected Elder."

"Correction. Guru. Do you remember when we decided not to fall for the guru club, Sarah."

"He better be worth it, is all I am saying." She has no idea, but Wit does not fit her criteria of worth it.

"It isn't about him. It's about me and choices. I don't know if I will choose to be his friend, but I need to know I am free to do so, here, in this house." Sarah stares hard at me like I was the biggest, most naive dope in the world.

"I can tell you right now, you're not." Her eyes well with tears.

"Maybe not, but I intend to push the envelope." I say. It is a struggle to look at her.

"Are you gay?" she asks.

"No."

"Then what is this about?" The business of choice doesn't sit right with her. I am not as sure about it as I want to be either.

"I don't know. I really don't. The promise is choices. I just want to push that as far as I can."

"You mean this in a direction kind-of-pathway kind of way don't you." Her eyes open wide.

"Maybe," I say, very nearly sorry already that I said it.

"Wow." She stands for a moment then says, "Okay, Will. I hold ground with you." I introduce Wit to each member of the family.

• • • •

My sweet mom has no idea Wit is gay. She thinks he is a nice young white boy. Pop sees it, my brothers see it, and even Uncle Eli sees it. The brothers find it amusing. Eli stiffens and Pop does not know how to respond. He sits there like a big old bear, moving his head from side to side, myopically trying to get a handle on what he is looking at. The guru, the one I call "Buster-Jesus-Christ-second-coming " sees it too. He goes into a tirade as soon as he figures it out. I am glad he mentions the "devil, evil and unnatural" in the same sentence. When he finishes I give him my most manly stare and reply, "There is no word for devil or evil in the Sto: loh language and neither you nor I is in a position to determine what is natural or unnatural about love and sex. That, I believe, belongs to the divinity of creation, not us." Pop suppresses a laugh. Tony can't, so he leaves the room. Momma ushers the good gentleman, Buster, out of the living room and into the kitchen for tea. He declines and leaves. Wit is horrified. He stands frozen to the spot. The light is definitely on him. Everyone stares at him.

"Focus boys," Sarah says and hands me a cape. We leave Wit standing there, wondering what he should be doing. He is still holding a cup of coffee. He drinks it, then relaxes. The bustle of everyone catches his attention.

"Is this what Miss Priss was talking about?" I am about to explain it all to him, but before I do, he tells me I don't have too. He knows his presence is making things a little tense, so he begs his leave. He goes and thanks Mom for the coffee, then tells everyone individually it was nice meeting them, using their names and goes out the door.

"Good memory," Sarah says quietly, trying to find some positive side to the mess I have just dumped onto the family floor.

"I will just say this, son. This is your mother's house. You will conduct yourself toward her visitors in accordance with her sense of courtesy. My suggestion to you would be to ask her if she thinks you did."

"Right now?"

"That would be my suggestion."

Mom is in the kitchen sewing studiously. "Was I out of line to you? Mom?"

"On which occasion? When you brought that boy home, or when you told Buster-Jesus-Christ-second-coming off?"

"How did you know I called him that?"

"I'm asking the questions now," she says good and crisp.

"When I told him off," I answer.

"Yes." It came out friendly, simple and short.

"I'm sorry."

"Well, you can just make that sorry a piece of reality. Clean out the house."

I turn to leave. She stops me. "What about the other occasion?" She is referring to bringing a gay man home.

"I'm about to become a man, Mom. If I am to have choices, I must have them here first. The choices, the freedom to choose my own path isn't real in the outside world, if it isn't real here. I was not, in my opinion, out of line at bringing him home. If I am, in your opinion, then I have no choices, in which case, I will not be showing up to the ceremony."

Where the hell did I get this? I am not sure I believe it. I sure as hell don't want to give up the ceremony. Just then lightning struck. The lights went out, Sarah must have sewed her own finger because I heard her scream, Mom stepped hard on the pedal of the sewing machine, and fortunately the power was out. Pop comes stumbling into the kitchen with a match. The lightning catches my mom's face; there are tears on her cheeks. Pop is scrambling for a candle. He finds one, lights it, then turns to me.

"Step out of your mother's house, before I get angry."

I step outside. The storm is amazing. I watch it as I watch my own insides become a family conundrum. Conundrum: an unsolvable riddle, a disappointment to the whole. Pale blue light-streaks silhouette the trees lining the edge of the road into our village. The houses appear blue-hued under the momentary light. The rain comes in great pelting drops; sheets of it. In seconds the yard is puddling up with water. The blue lightening shines electric on the landscape under the pelting rain. "*It is a crazed beginning Will, back off.*" I can't. Something happened to me. The crack of thunder is so close the sound seems to shake the house, the window behind me rattles. I can't back off.

Blue light floods the sky almost simultaneously with the boom of our Grandfathers. *I don't even know if I care about Wit anymore.* The blue streaks blink. I can't even explain it to myself. A softer flash of blue winks at the house. *It makes no sense, but I just have to make this thing real somehow.* A double boom from the Grandfathers affirms me. *I don't want a rubber stamp kind of ceremony.* Through the kitchen window, I see a jagged edged blue beams silhouetting my mom. *I want a real entrance to my own path.* Mom's tears stop. The crashing ancestral male voices subside, and begin to retreat. Mom's face is calm; she looks like she might reconcile herself to me. I take one more look at the storm receding back before I enter the house.

I'm standing in the kitchen doorway dripping. Rachel hands me a towel. Behind her I can see her baby on her back. She bends over something and her head disappears.

"What do you want from me?" Mom asks. She says it like she really wants to know.

"I want you to support whatever choices I make. I want to know you will love me, not because I fit into whatever preconceived molds you have cast for me, but because I am of you." It comes out humble, sandwiched between the faint booms of the retreating thunder.

The pale blue light follows her voice. Humbled by the Grandfathers, she whispers, "You belong to this lineage, this Clan, this family. You are entitled to your own path. I do not have to support you, but I will not stand in your way." The Grandfathers retreat. It's over. Tears are now rolling down my face. She retreats to the hall and sits down on the shoe bench. I move in her direction. Rachel turns around, smudge pot ready.

"This road you choose is strewn with sharp stones... do not expect me to anticipate it with ease. I believe choice is sacred and sometimes that butts up against my love for you, my fear for you. There are consequences for every choice you make. No one here wants you to choose the most difficult route to being." I stand behind her and knead the tension from her shoulders. I throw it out to the Thunderers and release my own fear at the same time. Tears sidle out from the outside corners of my eyes. Rachel dabs my face dry.

I don't really know this woman called my mother. Her touch is familiar, but not her being. We three watch the storm recede in silence. For fifteen years I have watched her work, heard the odd quip from her, seen her love my father in her looks, her small devotions, a clandestine touch when she believes no one is looking, but I have no idea how she thinks or what she thinks. I used to wonder what she thought about when I was small and I watched her during those hours of labour so tied to our living, our being. I know I have seen her mothering, felt its embrace like a soft folded full skirt and I have seen her as a new grandmother, but she is still such a stranger to me. My remark brought about near disaster. I wonder what made me think I could bring us all to the edge of calamity's cliff. The clap of thunder is now a whisper from far away. My hands rest on her shoulder gently. She reaches up puts her fingers on mine. My skin tingles at its gentleness, its fullness and I understand something about my father.

"I want a wife just like you Mom."

She turns sharply. Her hand gains weight, still keeping its delicate sweetness.

"You want a wife?"

"Yeah. Did you think?"

"I didn't know what I should think. I just had this picture of no grandchildren from you. And that was so sad."

I crack up. My mother's agenda is out in the clearing. She worked so hard during motherhood. I suppose she doesn't know me very well either. I picture her swallowing the desire to know her children, to have fun with them and promising herself grandchildren; not thinking that one of us might decline to produce children.

"You wouldn't mind me having a gay lover."

"Do you remember that serial killer? No, of course you don't. You weren't born. There was this serial killer and every day in court his mother was there, standing by him firmly, resolutely. I had such deep feelings for this woman. It would be so wrong to stand by your son if he had done those terrible things, but I could picture her son doing the so wrong thing and understand his mother feeling, like she had to stand by him."

"Mom. There is no parallel between homosexuality and serial killing."

"Except that people hate you for homosexuality in the same way."

A shiver ran through me. The lights went on. Pop strolls into the kitchen. He smiles.

"Don't move," he says. He reaches for the camera and takes a shot of us; me standing behind Mom, my hands still on her shoulders, her sitting looking up at me her hands on mine. He was smiling to beat the band. It dawns on me how simple my father is and how complex and mysterious my mother is. The guys in the living room are whooping it up, yak-yak-yakking about the storm, the Grandfathers and the thunder in men. I give my mom a peck on the cheek and nod at Rachel.

She hands me the bowl. I light it. She bathes herself with it. I pass it around the kitchen to Mom and Pop and head into the living room. About the middle of the hall Rachel leans into my face and says, "It's, Buster-Jesus-Christ-second-coming isn't it." I crack up as silently as I can. I can't move.

"Aren't you the one who showed your mom the correct way to do the arm thing?"

"Hush, Rachel. I can only stifle one laugh at a time."

"I know," she says so sweetly, it was magic. That's what Tony calls her, his magic woman. "Glad to have you in this family, sis." She strolls behind me and gives me a gentle nudge. I clean the whole house out with Rachel in tow. At the top of the stairs she wafts out the smoke and says, "Be gone, beast." This time I don't have to stifle my laughter. She looks at me, "Sometimes, Will, adults forget how cute we are."

"What do you mean?"

"Well, seems to me as an outsider, from the stories Tony tells, that you aren't any different today than the little guy who said 'be gone, beast' or properly showed your mom how to give you the fist. But now, with that large body of yours, it doesn't look so cute. They will get used to it and before long they'll be laughing about it again."

"Don't threaten me, sister."

She laughs and we head downstairs.

"It's Wednesday. Are we going to make it?" I ask everyone in the room.

"Not unless we work all night, either tonight or tomorrow night." Both George and Tony say it at once. "Owe me a Coke." Again at the same time.

"Up all night she is then," from Sarah. "We can't be tired on Saturday. But we can be tired at school."

There is a hard and chilly quiet in the air. I can feel the strain of it. Even the quilters who maintain a steady conversation on their own about babies, boyfriends and husbands are quiet. All heads are bent down as they sew furiously. All their heads, neatly parted at the top are all I see. Their long braids and their fingers, stitching, stitching and stitching. They are determined to absent themselves from this moment. Someone is going to say something here soon.

"So what's the scoop here?" The question comes from Tony.

"Yeah? You going to make us uncles or what?"

"Yeah. We made you an uncle. Well. Tony did. And I plan to too."

"This is the most self-interested family in the world. I bring a homosexual buddy home and all you care about is being an uncle to my progeny, all Mom cares about is being a grandma to my children. I could choose a woman who doesn't want children at all boys, did you think of that?"

"No. We didn't. Which is why we are asking." Tony just dropped it out, neat and flat.

"You have to put it in the yes or no form guys, other-wise you invite him to intellectualize," Sarah intervenes. She doesn't like testy conversations of more than three sentences going on between us. More than three sentences turns into an argument and you all start rutting and threaten-ing she says. "Do you, or do you not want children?"

"I don't know. I guess. Yeah. Yeah. I do. But more than children, I want to see the world, go to school and meet some loving woman."

"A woman is more important than kids?" Sarah asks.

"Yeah."

"And the world and school are more important than a woman?"

"No. They are just first in line because I am only fifteen."

Chapter 7

No dreams—just flower gardens, hysterical laughter about nothing, then around 7:00 a.m. shower, breakfast, and stagger for the bus. Mom fixes us all up with ginseng. My brothers are still at it when Sarah, Thomas and I leave. I feel for whoever is going to wear the breastplates they make today. They will be heavy if Gramma is right about putting your feelings into whatever it is you make. Tired makes me feel about six-years-old, except you weigh the same. I want to hold Sarah's hand again, troupe off to school half baby-talking, interrupting the conversation with dumb questions. I resist.

At school Thomas and I join Wit and the nerds. Wit knows things. He is talking about microbes, viruses, parasites, new diseases and clear cutting. He tells the story of Cedar. We were misbehaving about 10,000 years ago. "Off track" in modern parlance. The floods came, the animals died. Raven felt sorry for us. We were so sick and so fatigued. She called us together. We talked it up. Decided to get back "on track." Cedar agreed to hold the sickness of the Invisible People in the skirt of her roots. We would have to take care of her though, choose her death wisely. No clear-cutting. He ends it with, "Did you know that every day sixty new microbes are being let loose in the air by clear-cutting the Amazon rain forest." There is something in these stories.

"How do you know this story?" I ask.

"My Gramma lives with me."

"I know that," I answer.

"She is from Squamish Band."

"You're kidding?"

"No. Why, that makes me an almost Indian. If it was my granddad then I would be a card-carrying for sure Indian."

"What? You didn't know?" Phillip says.

"Why, we thought you joined us because you thought Wit was kin." He fakes some kind of accent like he's from Arkansas or some such. I look at Wit. I can see it now. He has cheekbones and ample cheeks. His eyes are brown. His brows are arched, slightly heavy and clearly defined. His hair is sandy, not blonde, and not brown, but this odd sandy colour. His skin is not really white either. And he has lips to pout with. The white guys I know don't have much in the way of lips, well, besides that older-than-dirt rock and roll star what's-his-name?

"No. I joined you because I thought you were nerds."

"Why, thank you. That reason for joining us is so much better. What do you think my fellow nerds, be proud boys, speak up. Up with nerds." Wit responds with his customary humor.

"Why would you want to hang out with nerds, white nerds, at that?" Paul asks.

"Nerds are thoughtful and I like that."

The jocks were moving this way. They were still stung

by Wednesday's cheek from me. They had regrouped. They were now moving in to raise the stakes.

No, I say to myself, we aren't going to do this. I rise from the table.

"Come on boys, we are going to visit the coach. Now! Before the jocks get across the caf." Paul, Wit and Joseph grab their books, look behind them and swing in behind me. Joseph is walking forward while looking behind so he bumps into me and says sorry. Nervously he swings in next to me, still walking forward and looking behind, he jostles my elbows.

"Joseph, walking works better when you look where you're going," Wit quips.

"Yeah, sorry." He looks forward.

We are walking pretty briskly. The jocks are jockeying their way through the crowd trying to get to us and I am praying I'll be right about the coach. I spent two years here watching everyone's movement. Teachers are creatures of habit. Every day the coach waits till the lunch crowd is in the cafeteria then he walks from the classroom to the bathroom, then to his office. If he is on schedule we should catch him before he gets inside his office. I am also praying the jocks are being cool and moving slow like jocks do.

"They are catching up," Joseph whispers to my shoulder. Now I am in a sweat.

"Sarah has her girlfriends blocking them," Wit says to my other shoulder.

"Where?" I say.

"In front of the door," Joseph answers.

"That should give us five seconds, it's all we need."

"Where are we going?" the quietest nerd asks. I don't even know his name.

"Just do what I say, exactly when I say it. Trust me," I answer. I can hear the exchange between the jocks and Sarah's girlfriends.

"Say excuse me," they tell them, blocking the way. It takes a few seconds for the jocks to give in.

"Okay, squaw, excuse us." They do. It hurts to hear them say that to Sarah.

"Shame on you," Kathleen barks at their receding backs. Cuss words follow from the jocks. They are at the end of the hall. We are at the front. I see the coach.

"Block their view of the coach when we get there boys." They do. He is stocky and short; the nerds are all tall. I am not so tall, but I'm taller than the coach and that is good enough. I ask the coach to just stand there for a minute while I explain what is going on.

"What is this about, Will?"

"You'll see, sir." A moment passes and the jocks arrive.

"Why, it's the fag gang. Are we blowin' someone? I got me a big red one." comes from behind.

The coach's eyebrows arc, he wants to look. I shake my head. He gets it. Then the push comes. I crash into the coach, my head gets him in the nose as I go down. His whistle goes off. The jocks freeze. The coach is on his feet bleeding. The jocks behind me see his blood and look like they want to die. Any violence and they are off the team.

"Who pushed Will?" the coach questions and all the traitorous little jocks point to Jack.

"Turn in your uniform." The others retreat slowly.

"I'm not done with the rest of you—to my office. You all wait there until I arrive."

He gets our story, then leaves to fix his nose. Jack is standing waiting to talk to me. He wants some kind of closure. I do too. I tell the others to disappear. They do.

"I'm prepared to ask the coach to let you back on the team, if you're prepared to tell your boys to make sport of football and not other humans."

His father is going to kill him for getting kicked off the team. "Bully anyone you want, but don't get caught," is his father's cardinal rule. I know his dad. He encouraged Jack all through grade school to bully me, but always with the dictum, "Don't get caught." Whenever Jack did get caught, his father became his personal private bully.

Jack's T-shirt is dampening under the armpits. His forehead is dotted with beads of sweat. His hands are twitching. He does not want to acknowledge the power I have at this moment, but he does not want to face his father as anything but a jock.

"Done deal." he shrugs.

"Sorry man. It isn't personal. I just got to have choices." He looks confused. Too deep for him I guess.

I arrive at the office about the same time as the coach. I talk to the coach for about ten minutes. The coach has always liked me. He knew the others gave me a hard time, calling me "Chief" and "Smoked Meat" and occasionally tackling too rough in practice. I have been injured more times by my teammates than our opponents. He tried to intervene, but unless they pushed me off the field there was not much he could do but encourage me to hang in there, scold the boys for their language and so on.

Jack comes up to me later.

"He suspended me." His fists are still clenched, but he leans against the locker like he is resigned to his fate.

"How long?"

"One week."

"Easy mush. Best I could do man."

"Yeah. He told me you had to do some fast-talking. Why man?" Jack is shuffling with his hands in his pockets now.

"Why to what? Why fast-talk the coach into keeping you? Why rat on you? Why hang out with the nerds? Why what?" I ask.

"Why did you talk to the coach?"

"I know your old man. He is going to beat the crap out of you for getting caught, right?" I say with empathy.

"What's that to you?"

"Look. I just want to live. Be let to live. Be let to be. I don't want to hurt anyone or make any waves. I just want the right to be."

Jack looks confused, but he accepts the answer. I check my books into my locker and head home.

Chapter 8

It's Thursday. One more evening, then blessed sleep. I don't have to go to school tomorrow—time off for ceremony. Mom can't believe it. Ceremony became a legal practice in her lifetime, now we are entitled to "time off" for it. I just hope the jocks of the world catch up to our new reality by the time my son hits the deck running in their direction. Sitting around our little tables, I say thanks to Sarah.

"Did you win?"

"Yeah," I reply throwing my fist in the air.

"Then be a gracious winner."

"What do you mean?"

"Treat Jack with respect."

"Even after he called you squaw?"

"It's a word... like fag... it doesn't mean anything to him. I don't mean anything to him. You don't either, but if you treat him right, you will mean something. Then maybe you can challenge his language."

"Like Great Grandpa did with Jimmy?"

"Yeah."

"What are you two talking about?" from Tony.

"Oh, big boy decided to go to war today. Got the nerds pushing back on the jocks. He won too."

"Ooh. Sounds juicy," George says.

But I interject, "If it weren't for Sarah, we would have lost badly."

"You remember that boy. You owe me—big time," she laughs.

I am about to get into the story when Sarah gives me her focus look. So, I have to recount it without all the blood, rush or the adrenal excitement I felt when I fought the battle and won. It was still more than okay.

• • • •

Between the flowers growing up in my garden of beads Gramma's back shows up. At first she's standing at the base of a hill. There is a stove on her back. She staggers up the hill. Behind her, her husband is grimacing. At first I think he is grimacing from the weight of his own load, but he isn't. He is seeing his beautiful little wife struggling up hill with a hundred pound load. Her legs quiver with the weight. Her feet find their footing carefully and tentatively; sometimes she hesitates. A horse in front stumbles. The line shifts to let him fall. The man tethered to the horse tries to untie himself—too late, they both fall screaming over the cliff's edge. The line stops. "Keep up! Keep up!" The foreman is screaming and jerking on the line.

There is no safety rope tethered to the long line of Indians going up this pass. They're packers. They are weighted with goods the horses can not haul. Unlike the white men and the horses, the Indians are considered dispensable by the foreman. Indians do not receive any protection against rolling down hill.

One stop in the front can send the whole line off balance. They need to keep moving. In some strange way, Grandpa seems glad his wife is not tethered to anything. Before long someone will again go catapulting downhill, stove, lumber, and sluice pans flying. If you aren't tethered you can sometimes jump out of the way. Not being tethered creates a different tension. If you do slip, you definitely die. The tethered only die if it is the horse that slips. Those who slip try to fall toward the canyon maw below to save their relatives. Grandpa had told his wife to remember if you fall, try to fall in the direction of the canyon. He hated telling her this.

• • • •

"Why are they there?"

"Where... who... what in the world are you talking about?"

It is out there. I said it out loud. I can't believe I said that out loud. Now I have to backdrop the question with a story. Maybe I can conjure the story without telling anyone that I was seeing it unfold as I beaded.

"I was just remembering the story of Great Gramma and Grandpa packing for the white men up there in Barkerville. I wonder how come they had to do that?"

• • • •

The picture changes. Fires beset our territory. Illness is everywhere. People perish in the wake of the arrivers. The fires kill our food source, the source of our nets and weirs we use to fish, the bark and roots we use for clothes and the timber of our homes. Money, they need money to trade for wood, for nets, for needles, for clothing, for homes...

Then I see Grandpa, and he speaks. "These people burned everything. The forest was our buffalo. Our food, our clothes, our tools all came from it. Naked, but for the clothes on our backs we left in search of work. They endangered our lives when we worked for them. 'The only good Indian is a dead one,' was the rule of law then. Those that weren't killed in the epidemics, died of starvation after the fires, died as packers, as road builders, as humans passing through a town. They just wanted us dead." He speaks this without even breaking the rhythm of his carving.

Grandpa feels his love leaking from the very sweat which constantly drips from his pores. He licks the love filled sweat as it rolls down his face, trying to hang on to his immense love for this small woman in front of him. He swallows it as he repeats his marriage vows over and over again. Every drop of sweat that crosses his mouth becomes a jewel of betrothal, of promise, of some kind of crazy hanging on. At night he prays to the stars, to the grasses, the winds, the four-legged, the winged, the ancestors, to the stone people, to every being he can name, to hold his heart safe from this icy, numb deadness he feels creeping into his bones. Every morning he wakes up just a little more morose than the day before.

They return home again. Rebuild the house; not as big as before. There are so few of them left. None of his wife's sisters survive and six of their twelve children perish, two of hers and four of his die. Their wild foods, *camas* and berries are gone, so they farm. They need a horse to saddle up and ride into the hills in order to find food. It is a long journey on an empty belly. Even after a generation, the food has never returned to the valley. Every day the river is bled of fish. Every day, a new mill is built in place of some dead village. Every day more disease-bearing settlers come. Every year some sickness threatens their survival, some job creates the terrible tension of pending death. Lapogee grows silent. His definition of love changes. Not all at once, but slowly. Work becomes its main expression.

• • • •

"Hard work killed us."

"Where are you boy?" Pop says, but he knows where I am. "No. Hard work saved us, those people were trying to kill us, still are, as far as I'm concerned. Hard work helped us to survive, some of us anyway. Those people killed us. They wanted us dead. Never forget that," Pop says.

"Do you think we could change the subject? I mean you're putting that into those little gardens of yours and some girl is going wear it," Sarah says.

"What did we do before white men brought beads?" I ask, changing the tone of things.

"We didn't do anything after they brought beads," Tony says with skip-jump-raven-push kind of laugh, "least not till recently."

"What do you mean?"

"Baby, you are young," Sarah teases.

"You mean, what did the Crees do before beads?" George throws his oar in the water.

"What's a Cree?" I ask. Everyone laughs then.

"Another kind of Indian," Sarah answers.

"They did these beautiful flower patterns with dyed moose hair and porcupine quills on hide shirts and dresses. When white people brought beads, they used beads."

"What did we put on our shirts?"

"Nothing," Pop says, "we didn't wear shirts."

George and Tony let go a pair of "Whoops!"

"Bare breasted. Even the women?" George asks. Pop nods yes.

"Bring back the good old days," Tony and George holler. Both Tony and George carry on about a real garden, a garden of bare breasted women. The quilters come alive. They squeal with modest excitement at the thought of them marching about with no shirts, sewing on this floor, in this room, with these men watching, their breasts bobbing with the motion of pulling on thread, cutting and re-threading. It is too much for them.

"You wouldn't feel that way if you were alive back then, stupid. You'd be used to it." Sarah is clearly miffed. Pop chuckles. Even he doubts that. This gal has no idea how visual men are. A breast, a glimpse of one, even the memory of one can get us going. Pop hasn't got tired of the same pair, day after day, night after night and year after year. We make songs out of the pair of breasts awaiting us at home. Of course, any of us would die before we would admit this to our girl relatives.

"'I once asked your grandpa how he kept from losing the love of his life, as he watched her do more than a man's work?' He told me: 'She did a workhorse's work. Those people reduced us to animals, I looked at her breasts in my mind,' and then he laughed." Pop says as he too laughs.

"Yup, that would about do it for a man. No. That wasn't it. The breasts in your village were the breasts of your relatives. Your breasts better not excite the men in this room, honey." Pop says to Sarah. Sarah sticks her tongue out at him.

"So, when did we start doing this?" I ask, gesturing to my beadwork.

"In the '60s. When the Crees came." Sarah answers.

"Came to where. There are no Crees around here."

"Vancouver."

"So you and your mom brought this here?"

"Yeah," she says, tossing back her pretty head.

"Cool." It is nice to know. I think about it and figure it makes sense. There are very few wild flowers around here; just the white ones and barely pink ones that form the fruit blossoms on berries, bushes and vines and crab apple trees. Not much to imagine gardens with. There must be daisies and roses and all kinds of flowers on that prairie. This makes sense to me. All that flat land would have to be interrupted and spotted with beauty or everyone would die of boredom and leave. Here there are mountains to hold, to cradle your sense of civilization.

I focus on the room. The women in the corner are back into their comfortable meander around their small worlds of mothering babies.

"Justin is walking. He looks like Charlie Chaplain."

"In fact, that is where Charlie got the idea of that little tramp walk," someone says, "from watching babies learn to walk."

"I shot a video of Justin. It's funny," Justin's mom says. "Oh. Have you got it here, let's look at it," another replies.

She takes it out of her bag. I cannot believe women and their bags. They are ready for anything. They need something, they just open up the bag. Once the car broke. Pop needed a screwdriver. Mom dipped into her bag. She did not have a screwdriver, but a bread and butter knife from her bag did the trick just the same. I begin to believe that women plot the day out, carefully orchestrating its unfolding and dump things into their bag to help the story along.

The video gets plugged into the video machine and soon Justin is up there on the screen. With his back facing the camera, Justin staggers and makes his way over to his pop. His mom is shooting the film. His gramma, my Auntie Lillie, is encouraging him, spotting for him in case he loses his balance. He is on the front lawn. The grass is cruelly uneven. He begins to tip backward, waves his little arms in a circular motion and gurgles a funny sound. This uprights him somehow, then he lists to the right, his left arm twirls and he is centered again. He steps three more steps then throws himself at his pop, turns and gives one of those winning smiles to the camera. We all laugh and replay the video. We carry on about how cool this film will be when Justin finds his first love.

"Ah, you guys," his mom, says.

"We can hardly wait," I say.

"Imagine the first time he brings that gal home and he is being all cool, then we put on the movie and all she can say is, 'Ah, cute,'" George says imitating one of the women saying that about him as we watch.

"What you doing, boy?"

I look down at my cape. Again, it wasn't anything like Sarah's barrette, not even close. It was a garden of tiny wild violets; forget-me-nots and pearled baby's breath; its thin green leaves of all colours peering through deep forest are contrived of near black green pearl beads. It was beautiful, but nothing like the barrette.

"I do not know," I say, "seems like as soon as I said the word flower gardens in my mind, my fingers, just started doing whatever they wanted. I'm sorry."

"Ha-ay," Millie, my second cousin, says. "That looks like my mom's patch of wild flowers underneath our cedar tree."

I am grateful it looks like something, but beside myself about how I am going to stop beading whatever comes to my fingers.

"Well, maybe it's better if I try to match your capes, then for you to match my barrettes, since you can't seem to stay focused," Sarah laughs.

Mom appears and looks at Pop. Pop disappears, comes back a minute later and looks at Tony; Tony disappears with Pop. A few minutes later Mom appears and looks at George and me. We disappear with her.

We go outside with Mom and she tells us, Anne's friend from the city is coming in. "We can't have a guest sleep on the floor and these women are going to stay until the works done, then sleep here for a couple of hours, then work some more. Pop is going to go outside and throw up the tent. You boys will have to sleep out there to free up the rooms."

"Sure," we agree at the same time.

"Owe me a Coke." Again at the same time. Within seconds of all this appearing and disappearing, we are all back in the room except for Pop. Sarah is already working to make a barrette to match my mistake. I start another garden.

Chapter 9

My Great Aunt Bessie is still alive. She is so old she barely gets around, but she used to be a live wire. She liked to party all her life. Not too long ago, Tony, George and Callie took her bar hopping. She has a garden too. Daisies, opium poppies and echinacea, all grow in her garden. The soil around it is sandy. Black round stones circle the garden. I love the purple, magenta and pinks of the echinacea against the yellow and red of the daisies and black centered red poppies. The leaves of Aunt Bessie's flowers are all similar; long pale green slivers cutting through the light. After a good rain they glisten in the sun and unfurl their leaves looking like they just took a long much-needed drink of water.

"Remember, the poppy is also a flower," Uncle Eli says. It sounds kind of odd. We have no idea what the set up was, but he says it like is some punch line from some memory, so we laugh. We are about the only humans in the world I know that'll laugh at a punch line without knowing the set up. Eli chuckles along with us without explaining the source of the joke. Doesn't matter. We are all feeling so tight, so tired and so good about what we're doing.

We used to live like this a hundred years ago. Big old Longhouses made of cedar with a common working area and benches all around the house. Private quarters up higher. I figure some piece of us hungers for this, cause we keep fixing our ceremonies so that we don't have time to just fiddle faddle around in our own homes. We all gather and go into crisis mode at the house of whomever's ceremony it is and work our fingers to the bone for about a week, laugh our heads off, tease the life out of each other and somehow it all falls into place.

Jay is sorting through the stuff in the chest, marking who is to receive which item. Every now and then she takes a minute to admire the work. "Good one, cousin," rolls out. She comes across Momma's rose garden cape and gasps.

"This is too much. Man, I want my son to love me this much." A little tear escapes from her eye.

Women from the kitchen are drawn to the living room like a magnet to her soft words. But they could not have heard that all the way from the kitchen, they must have felt it. Whatever drew them in here, they all begin whispering how beautiful the beaded garden is.

"Sarah, this is gorgeous," Anne says.

"He did it." Sarah looks towards me.

"That's my boy," Mom says and goes back to the kitchen, Anne in tow shaking her head saying, "Why, Mary that's your rose garden to a tee... to a tee."

"Ain't that something... ain't that something," follows from the lips of Lilly and Jenny.

Jay sets it aside. She doesn't want to decide who it's for until she has all the rest tagged. Callie disappears and returns with a camera. She takes a shot of all the artwork lying out in the middle of the floor. There is a stack of quilted blankets in the corner. Once Jay and Callie have the trunk stuff all tagged, they lay the blankets out on the floor, photo and tag them. They all have ribbon shirt edges and trellises of flowers quilted in columns next to the edges, then geometric diamond or triangle or sea wave quilting in the middle. The colours are unbelievable.

Every piece gets an 'ooh' and 'ah' from anyone who sees them. They are all trimmed kind of like a pillowcase, with a slip of satin edging all around. The back of each quilt is all the same. An ashberry coloured cotton sheet. Ashberry is Mom's favorite colour. It is a mauve kind of pink sheeting.

Jay tags each one, carefully folds them up. Callie leaves after taking photos and returns with a bunch of bags. They are really nice bags, blue-green, turquoise and gray. Southwest Native geometric designs with Northwest colours. They are big—big enough for the blankets to fit inside them. She holds them out and Jay tucks each blanket in. It is going to be quite the Give Away.

"Oh, look. Isn't that going to be just too modest? They are going to have to take it out themselves to look at it."

The women giggle. "Your mom is so smart." And they laugh some more.

"You're wanted on the phone, Will." Auntie Anne says to me. Sarah looks up. I shake my head and shrug as I tiptoe through the blankets spread out on the floor.

"You not coming to school tomorrow, Will?"

"No." It was Wit. How did he get my number? We aren't in the book and I sure never gave it to him.

"Miss Sassafras, gave me your number. She asked me to phone and tell you I would be bringing by your work. I did point out that 'time off for ceremony' for white folks, means no work in church, so to speak. She looked like she was going to cry, like she was feeling she was never going to get this white person relating to an Indian business right, so I let her off the hook and told her I would bring you your work. If you don't feel like doing it, don't worry about it. They don't give us homework over the Christmas holidays, if you catch my drift." He is laughing at all his own jokes. I guess he is more than an almost one of us. At least he got that part right anyway—laughing at his own jokes. Maybe I do like him.

"You know Will, my aunt and cousin are coming to town. They say they will be at your place till Sunday. You know anything about that?"

"I just know my Auntie Anne lived in Vancouver for ten years or so, her best friend and daughter from Van are coming here."

"Must be them. Maybe we'll be relatives after all someday."

"What do you mean?"

"You'll see. I'll be by tomorrow." Turkey, he hung up. No sense thinking about it. I go back to work. I lay down the phone and ask Auntie Anne where her friend's from.

"North Van," she says.

"Squamish Band?" I ask.

"Yeah, you know her? Her mom's sister lives here with her daughter somewhere, Chilliwack I think, maybe Sardis."

"I think she's Wit's cousin," I answer, looking at my mom.

"Whose Wit?" Anne asks, also looking at my mom as though I had just left.

"Isn't Wit that white boy?" She asks me, ignoring Anne.

"Well Lani says her gramma married white and so did one of the sisters," Anne says, again like I am not there.

"I think the one that lives out here did marry out." she is talking to herself now. I don't want to confuse the air in the room so I leave.

"Who's Wit?" Anne insists on knowing. I can hear my mom telling her about my new friend Wit as I saunter down the hall and try to picture his cousin. I am catching on to the call. Wit is a pretty looking guy. He reminds me of a pale skinned Hawaiian poster girl—almost. I go back down the hall to the kitchen.

I have to ask, "How old is her daughter?"

"Don't you even go there, boy. You are not a man yet. You won't be after this ceremony either. You have four more years and a Winter Dance to go through before you even think about that."

"Fifteen," Auntie Anne mouths and winks at me.

"Hush, you. Don't get him started."

"He must have his daddy's blood," Anne giggles and the women both laugh in that naughty giggle kind of way. As I walk back toward the living room again, I am wondering how they are going to get here. There is no bus service to any reserve in the world that I know of, except North Van's Squamish Band. Maybe they don't know that. I go back to the kitchen.

"Don't you have some work to do?" Momma says.

"How are they getting here?" I ask.

"Oh, isn't that sweet. He's worried about them," Anne gives Momma a nudge.

"You are so dead, Anne, if you don't let up," Mom scolds.

"Car, honey. They are coming by car," Anne assures me, paying no attention to her elder sister's threat.

Around 10:00 p.m., about the time I finish Aunt Bessie's garden, I hear a car. My heart stops. What if she is beautiful? What if she is light like Wit? I don't want some light-skinned Native. I want one like the song "Prettybrown."

I wonder about courtship. I stab myself a good one with a needle. Sarah gives me a "What's up with that?" kind of look. Anne enters the living room looking triumphant. There is no imagination that can conjure a woman as beautiful as her friend. She has a brilliant drop-dead beautiful smile. She is slender and moves like she's walking on water. She looks to be around thirty-five years old, but has the kind of face you know is going to be gorgeous forever. She is the most beautiful woman in the world. Then her daughter slides in behind her. My eyes hurt. Something else is beginning to ache too. Some piece of me that until now has been only functional, even an occasional pain in the butt has just woken up. I lay the cape down in my lap. Both my brothers laugh. They know what's going on. I want to die. I have to look again. I look up grinning from ear to ear.

"Will, why don't you show Lani and her daughter to their room?" My aunt is so wicked, she borders on cruel.

As I stand up to show them upstairs, I step on the thread to my own needle, it stops my feet but my upper body keeps going. I land nearly in the laps of the two women. They step back and catch me then smile politely, like this must be our traditional Sto: loh welcome.

"We're so honoured to be here," slides out of Lani's lips, sultry and lyrical.

"Sorry," I manage to mumble while I drop the cape.

"That's a Sto: loh boy's way of saying we're honoured to have you," George says, and he and Tony laugh. Bastards. Her daughter winks. I don't know her name. I lead them up the stairs. I can't believe what a goof I have become. I stop about halfway up to see if they are still coming and of course they are, so Lani bumps into me. I say sorry, then like seven different kinds of a fool, I do it again.

"We will follow you Will, you just lead the way." She is so polite. She doesn't want to say, 'straighten up, boy.' She has the politeness of a woman who knows the effect she has on men. She also knows her daughter has the same magic. If it's possible she is a younger, prettier version of her mom. She isn't light though, so Lani must have married another Indian. That makes her too much. I can't stop grinning. I manage to make it through two flights of stairs.

At the door, I pause again. They bump into me, I apologize, I can't for the life of me think of a reason not to let them in, but I do not want to open the door. I have to open the door.

"Is there something wrong, Will?" Lani purrs.

"No." I open the door and casually, but quickly I explain that they can use the bottom drawer for their personal things. I tell them the window is old and show them how it works, where to find the stick to hold it up, if they want it open. I point out the alarm clock and show them how to set it. Finally, I say the clean sheets are on the night table. They could see that. I turn to leave, hoping neither of them looks at the wall. That way I won't have to apologize for the wall posters. I could shoot myself for having such bad taste. Once some guys made an "Indian calendar," you know for boys. Every Indian Nation's women got on their case about this particular year's calendar, so they toned the next ones down after that. The gals are dressed skimpy and wearing inviting looks on their faces. March is still up and it's early June. Not that it matters, since the year is wrong too. Of all the women, March is the least dressed. I want to change it, but it would be so tacky. I want to tear it off the wall but that would mean I would have to face my guilt and embarrassment. I am almost out the door, when I hear it.

"Oh, she's very pretty," the young one says and gives me a naughty, naughty, finger-wagging kind of look.

"March... isn't it June?"

"Well, it's also the year 2000 and the calendar I believe says '96, doesn't it, Will?" her mother asks. I take if off the wall and apologize.

"Oh. You can leave it if you like. Just in case we get confused about what day it's not." Lani smiles a wicked grin. Her daughter laughs slightly. I swallow. If I get through this weekend with any dignity at all left, I believe I will be a man.

I get down the stairs, everyone is quietly working, not a good sign.

"Yep. Uncle Eli's right—men are visual," Sarah starts.

"And that was some visual, hey bro." They are on a roll. Tony rises and says with huge flourish, "Shall I give you the Sto: loh man's traditional welcome. First, I stab myself with a beading needle, then I step on my beading thread, then crash into the female guests, finally I drop my cape." He performs each act as he talks.

"And then, when they express their honour at the invitation to our Potlatch, I say 'Sorry,' like it was some kind of terrible mistake." Tony barely gets this out, he is laughing so hard, and spit is dribbling down the side of his mouth. Sarah stops beading, she is laughing so hard.

"Puts a whole new meaning to the phrase falling in love." Callie has left the kitchen to join the fracas.

Jay has to leave the room and head for the bathroom.

"I didn't think it was possible, Will. But this is better than the bike," George tells me, which means they can all get much more mileage out of it. I would want to kill them if I weren't laughing so hard. Fatigue brings on hysteria in some form, hysterical anger, and hysterical sad or hysterical laughter. We are so fatigued we can't stop. Mom comes in with the spray bottle and shoots us all in the face a couple of times with ice water before we can recover.

"Focus," she says and leaves, chuckling away to herself. Every now and then Eli gets us going again. The women in the kitchen are laughing good and hard too, likely about the same thing. Difference is, the women can work and laugh at the same time, and us guys can't seem to. We finally settle down about midnight. We finished what we started around 2:00 a.m., and then we just couldn't do it anymore. Just then Mom appears.

"Turn in boys, it's a long day tomorrow." Every line on Mom's face is showing and her shoulders sag. Every thing is hanging just a little lower than usual. My mom is fifty. Her eyes are as warm and happy as ever, but her body has about had it with kids. Twenty-seven years of us and now she is in the home stretch.

She has one of Callie's babies in her arms. She strokes the baby's hair and gives her such a sweet look. I picture her looking at each one of us like that, stroking our hair, and getting ready for ceremony after ceremony, year after year. After I am grown up, things will change. She will be like Gramma, sitting in the corner making whatever she feels like. Staying up till she feels like turning in, then just going to bed not worrying about what's done and not done, just going to sleep in Grandpa's arms. Gramma always had one of us sleeping on her ample lap. She still does. The one Momma is now holding is snoozing away on Gramma's till she turns in. Momma lays the child on a blanket in the kitchen until she is ready to take her up to bed with her. Callie and Tony's gal Rachel clean up the mess the women made in there.

Chapter 10

We are in the tent. The sound of country quiet all around; crickets, frogs, dogs and coyotes pierce the soft tree muffled world every now and then. The guys giggle into their blankets about my antics earlier, but don't carry on. They are savoring the memory, playing with what they can do with it later.

"So," George says after a quiet time, "how'd they like the calendar?"

"The calendar?" Tony asks.

"Right. You are too old to know about the calendar." George is laughing.

"1996 almost skin Indian pin-up calendar." I help Tony along.

"It was still up?"

"He didn't buy it for the dates?" They laugh. They kept trying to get out of me what happened when the women saw the calendar, but I didn't bite.

"What goes on in the bedroom is no one's business," I finally tell them. They leave it alone.

"Tony?" I ask, "How did you court Rachel?"

"Don't go there, boy, you a long way from manhood."

"I just want to know."

"I have known Rachel since second grade. Wasn't much of a courtship. I think I was in fifth grade when I decided she was the one. I just waited. When I was about seventeen she took up with this young man. I went over to her house. She seemed happy enough to see me. Then, she told me it was Friday, which I knew, and that she had a date with her young man. I asked her why she wanted to go and do that. 'Well, he likes me,' she said. 'I am glad you said that,' I said. 'Why?' she said. 'Because you didn't say you liked him.' 'Well, I like being taken out on dates,' she said. 'Okay' I said. 'I can do that.' 'Yeah?' she said. 'Yeah,' I said. 'Now why would I do that instead of dating him?' she said. 'Because you don't want him standing between us like an old ghost on our wedding night,' I said. She giggled, then left, made a phone call, then told me I was committed to taking her out."

"Why that's plum romantic, big brother, why didn't I think of that?" George says.

"What, you interested in someone specific, George?"

"Yeah, she is a Chehalis gal. They have them big eyes. Just can call the deep from within you. I just have no idea how to approach her. I want to go to college. I will just ask her to go there with me. She is old enough. Yeah. That is what I am going to do. Tomorrow."

"Tomorrow? She is coming here tomorrow? For the ceremony?" I ask.

"Yeah. You invited her, Will."

"Sarah's friend? Tina?" I ask.

"One and the same," George says.

"You a virgin George?" I ask.

"Yeah. Most guys my age are, bro. They just behave like they aren't. Most gals are scared. The ones that do indulge early end up with kids too soon. If they end up with kids too soon, the father is always someone who doesn't care about them. You got to care about kids, bro. To care about kids, Pop says you got to care a lot about women. I can see that. When I look at Tina, I don't see children, I see her and me. Now I know if I have my way there will be children some day, so I got to get used to that by caring about her."

"You got to like their moms too. Get to know them and pray their moms like you. Cause Indian women stick with their moms. Best you treat them right. Rachel comes with a truckload of girl cousins, aunts, sisters and her mom. If I get out of line they are all over me in a minute. That's why you got to go slow, bro. Go slow through life. Don't be in too much of a hurry to do the man thing." Tony says.

"How long you date Rachel, before... you know."

"That's none of your business, boy. It isn't about when that happened. It is more about when we decided to set up house together, to get married. It was after I graduated from college. On grad night I asked her to marry me soon. She said she wanted kids right away. I sucked wind and said soon as I get working, and apply for my own house on the reserve, we are going to get married. Lo and behold if those three things didn't come right away. By September there I was, married, paying a mortgage and getting ready to be a dad."

"Which goes to show, misery does come in threes," George says. We laugh.

Rachel walks around with her baby on her back. She goes to work at the daycare with her. She was in the kitchen sewing with her daughter on a cradleboard. That baby is never far from her mom. If Rachel tires, she hangs her baby on the wall. The baby is three months old now.

"What's to get ready about being a dad?"

"You disappear till the baby gets walking. I mean, you married this woman so you could be with her all the time and then, bingo, she's always with that baby. It's a shock, if you don't get some fair warning from the old guys about it. Pop says he married Mom to be with her all the time and that was about the end of that. He believes he saw her more during courtship then all the rest of the years put together after they married. Somewhere about five years into the marriage Pop decided he better do something to make a living that he really loved, because he was just as without Momma as he could be with kids and all. That's when he started carving. Mom says she didn't care how he put meat on the table or paid the mortgage, just 'sos he did. It was the same with Rachel. I get to watch her giving loving looks to this little girl that by some crazy miracle I fathered. I wake up in the night feeling frisky and there is this little short person sleeping between us." Tony rolls his eyes.

"Rachel says she falls asleep during the night feeding. I suppose it was the same with Mom and Pop. I do recall you crawling in with them long after she quit nursing you too."

I laugh. I remember that. I would be tap, tapping at the door, Pop would grumble some ugly sound, but Mom would be there, scooping me up and tossing me between them. Pop would make another grumpy sound and turn his back on me as I curled up with Mom."

"When was that?" George says, "last week?" and we laugh some more.

"How did Pop meet Mom?" I ask my brothers.

"Hopyards," Tony offers.

"Hopyards?" I repeat.

"They would go pick hops in July—whole bus loads of Native people. This whole valley used to be hops. Mom said to me once, 'imagine they grow fewer hops and make more beer? How do they do that?' I told her it was from chemical aging. *No wonder everyone gets crazed when they drink. Never use to be like that.* She shook her head and told me the story of how her and Pop met. He has another family you know."

George and I gasp. "Kids?" we both ask.

"Yeah. Out in Washington somewhere. The mom got TB and died. The gramma figured it was best she keep the kids and for Pop to just move on. Mom told me it broke his heart, to leave his kids, but he agreed. Every now and then he stares off into space and she asks him if he's thinking about them. He admits it. He was pretty young when he had them, nineteen he says, and twenty-eight when he left them. He's sixty-three now so they must be pretty old."

This stuns George and I, we are barely breathing throughout the rest of the story.

Tony continues, "Mom was seventeen. Pop started to carve himself a flute. Took him nearly half the season. Then one day he starts playing it underneath her cabin window. She pokes her head out, and calls her mom. Gramma comes to the window and tells him to come 'round on payday with that thing. He worked logging, then he'd go down to her village, this village, every break in the season for about two years. Finally he asked Gramma if he could marry Mom. Gramma said, 'yes, if she'll have you.' Mom said yes and that was that."

"That's sure different," I say, "I mean. I can't exactly ask a woman to go pick hops so I can make a flute and marry her." We laugh.

"Things have sure changed for us," George muses. "Grandpa and Gramma had an arranged marriage, Pops was pretty near to that. I guess ours is the first generation that is really out on its own. It's just like them people to end arranged marriages, but not tell us how to work the free choice system." George laughs.

"I don't think white guys are instructed on how to do it either. Everyone is just winging it," I offer.

"If you think that, you'd be wrong. I heard my friend Daniel's pop, Art, giving him instructions on how to go about dating, when he upped his allowance and encouraged him to try for his driver's licence, get a summer job and buy a car, all in one breath."

"Yeah?" I can't believe anyone actually sits and teaches their sons how to date. It just sounds too personal. I don't say that though. Maybe because it's their culture, it isn't personal.

"It's their way," George says. "I mean, we have no problem talking about the ceremony you're having, how to go about becoming a man. Just courtship isn't part of the original instructions because that was all arranged. The flute making and playing was the way you let the Elders know about your desire, then they arranged it. They leave that out, because most know the context is missing. Everything has changed. We just haven't figured out how to catch up with the change," he finishes.

"Thanks guys."

The dark gets denser as I slip into dreams. I dream I wake up. Great Grandpa is sitting on the edge of my bed.

I hear him speak clearly, "Everything is different now son. You're like the last autumn leaf floating in the wind, that hasn't quite yet fallen asleep. The hopyards are gone, the roads are built, and the skyscrapers are all done. Now it's just working with what's there. Everything is different but your insides are the same. Our laws don't change just because the landscape does. You figure it out in the same respectful way we do everything, *don't make any changes without ceremony* is all you have to remember." Poof and he is gone. It is dark and I am cold. My hands start to shake. I am awake. I pinch myself to make sure I really am awake. I pinch too hard, it hurts.

Great Grandpa, he was there. How did I know it was him? It is pitch black now. The spirit must have its own source of light I decide. Just remember what he said, *"Don't do anything different without ceremony."* No, that wasn't it. *"Don't change my insides without ceremony."* Which was it. *"The landscape has changed but not our insides."*

I rethink Tony's story about getting to know Rachel's mom, her sisters, her aunts, her girl-cousins. It's like he belongs to them now. That makes sense. A long time ago,

Tony would have had to move to Chehalis, now he just spends almost all his weekends there and when he isn't there, half of Rachel's female relatives are here. She went home to have the baby. They both stayed at Chehalis for a month. Tony had to drive back and forth to work from there. It added an hour to his workday. The men still belong to the women's family. *Don't change anything inside.* So where was Lapogee from in the first place? 'Shut up and go to sleep' I listen to the sounds of the night and the cool wind whispering across the tent. I am gone.

• • • •

6:00 a.m. seemed to crash up on us way too soon and much too violent. I jump up before I am even awake. I step on Tony, who cusses. A voice calling me to attention is unfamiliar.

"Easy boy, she'll still be here when you actually wake up." Tony and George crack up.

"Your mother says breakfast is ready." From outside the tent. It's her. There is a sweet rasp in her throat. All the Indian girls I know have voices with a lilt, but hers is a little deeper and has some kind of sweet scrape across the higher vocal chords as it rolls out at you. I want to hear that sound forever.

"What?" It's a dumb question, but that would be me: Dumb Question Will.

"Your mother says breakfast is ready." She ends the ready on a higher note; the way English indicates a question. I hear the grass crunching and swishing. She is leaving. I want to run out after her, fall in next to her, just so I can smell her, listen to the grass under her feet swish and crunch as she walks, maybe side-glance the top of her head, her body's profile as she moves.

I breathe. Still wearing the same clothes as last night, I head out of the tent and jog through the yard into the bush. Maybe a good hard run will help. Mom does not like us to be late for breakfast, but there is enough of a lineup for Josie's food for me to go ahead and run without being too late.

I am back within a half-hour. I'm right. The last of the men are filling their plates as I stroll in towelling the sweat off.

"Good idea," Pop whispers and touches my arm. He knows what's going on and I want to die, because Pop is always the last to figure things out, which means my girl cousins, my brothers, and this unnamed girl all know what is happening to me. When she leaves I am going to take such a ribbing. But, nothing happens for now, there is just the usual breakfast conversation.

On the run I had made up my mind to be friends with her, to try and see her as a woman the way I see my cousin, Sarah. She is so beautiful and I feel so very plain. I can't think of a single exciting thing about me.

She moves about the room like she is skating on some air pocket. From the end of the kitchen, she holds up a coffee cup. I nod.

"I want you boys to stop by Zellers and get some spare things. Just in case extra guests come. Things you can use in your own houses. Sheets, pillow cases, towels, stuff like that," Mom instructs us.

"We don't have enough?" I ask aloud.

"I think we do. But you never know. Someone is bound to bring some extra person along. I don't want anyone going home empty handed."

"We could make..."

"I want you out of the house today."

No one says why, but I bet it's because she doesn't want me mixing it up with Lei-Lani. Even her name is a song. Lei-Lani knows too. She looks over, gives me a "too bad" kind of look and starts washing up the dishes.

"You don't like sewing either, honey?" Josie asks.

"Oh yes, I do. But I like doing dishes too," she says and smiles at Josie. That smile, I want to see that smile every day. Josie heads for the shower, tells Lei-Lani she'll be right back.

The rest of the guys are packing up our work and getting ready to head for Zellers. The women are in the living room; there are so many more blankets to quilt. I am still eating. She walks over holding the coffee pot. My face is even with her breasts. I close my eyes, then look up, anywhere but at that chest.

"Warm up?"

"Sure. So you're Wit's cousin?" I ask.

"You know my cousin, Wit?"

"We just recently became school chums," I tell her.

"Oh." she says it soft and careful. I would have said more, but she retreats to her dishwashing and no more exchanges happen after that. I walk up behind her with my plate and slide it gently into the sink.

"He says you'll be visiting him on Sunday."

"Yes," she says. Her voice changes. I look at her. She doesn't look back. I accept it. I can't do this, anyway we are too young, but I had hoped we could be friends.

We do the Zellers thing. "Spend $300.00," Mom had said. That is a lot of sheets, pillowcases and towels. The guys pick the things they think their sister, aunt, cousin or wife would like. We decide to eat lunch at a local greasy spoon.

"She likes you, Will," Tony says it so dead serious. He is worried.

"I don't know," I answer, "she didn't even look at me after I started talking to her this morning."

"Oh-oh," from George.

"What did you say to her?"

"That I knew her cousin, Wit."

They crack up. "You are one naive little puppy. She probably took that to mean you were trying to hint that you were..." and he flicks his wrist.

"Well, maybe it's all for the best, Will. You are a long way from being a man."

"I know. But I wouldn't mind hammering down my interest; getting to be her friend."

"Oh yeah, right."

On the way back we pick up chips, movies, pop and other such. I am determined to talk to Lei-Lani. I walk into the kitchen. She is sewing.

"I would like to talk to you." I look into Lei-Lani's eyes.

"I believe you have other things to do," my mom tells me.

"No, actually, I don't. Two minutes, Miss Lei-Lani—on the front porch."

Lei-Lani frowns and looks to her mom, who nods 'yes'. My mom is still in shock.

Outside, the moon is full, just my luck. She is in front of me.

"I'm not what you think I am. I am Wit's friend. I know he is gay, but I am not interested in him in that way."

She smiles, gets all coy.

"I am interested in you," I tell her, "but I can't play house with you just like that. Do you know what I am talking about?" She nods.

"I want to be friends first. I am only asking one thing. You get a hankering for some other guy, tell me before you decide to do anything. Will you do that?"

"I am only fifteen, Will. I would like to be your friend. But, what if I just want to go on a date with someone?"

"Tell me."

"Okay."

We go inside. I feel invincible.

We check everything out. We are ready. Mom stands at the entrance to the living room. Everything is packed up. She has bags for every single thing. There are around 100 bags packed. Each one is slightly different than the other. Each one is slightly different in size, but basically all the same shape. In every bag there is a can of salmon and a jar of jam, along with whatever else we are giving away. Mom surveys the lot.

"It looks like we're done," Mom says to Jay.

"Except for your rose garden, Auntie," Jay says.

Momma looks at me like she is wondering who I am. I want to tell her I don't know myself. Things are roaring around in my mind a million miles an hour. I have no idea what to think about anything. I just know that I love being here in this moment, this time, at the tail end of this generation and in this family.

"Hello, Will. I believe Jay already told you that, you'll have to decide who gets the rose garden."

"It's your garden, Mom." It comes out real tender, much more than I intended it to. The room softened, the air gets lighter, and Lei-Lani got a little shy.

"You decide," I tell mom.

"I'll dream on it." She plays with a small stone in her hand, twirls it, tosses, pockets it in her apron and heads up the stairs for bed.

This time she doesn't tell us to turn in. She just calls the little ones. They troupe up the stairs after her, grabbing her skirt as they go. Pop falls in line. He casts a look at Callie as he leaves.

"Okay boys, let's turn in. We got a lot of work to do tomorrow." The shift is so smooth. Callie is in charge now.

Heading out to the tent I look up to see Grandma Moon in the night sky, looking like she is smiling down on us big and pale orange. Earlier she was huge and brilliant orange, now she is shrinking and her colour is fading. We stand out there staring at her for a while; Tony drops some tobacco. George and I follow suit. Inside the tent I can tell Tony and George want to say something.

"So, what did you tell her?" Tong begins.

"Something between what you said."

"Between what I said? I don't know if you see how little sense that makes, Will."

"Well, from inside what you said then."

"I have no idea what you are talking about, so just tell me what you said."

"I told her I wanted to be friends, but that I was wanting more in the long run, and that if she got a hankering for someone else, I wanted her to tell me. She agreed to it."

"Do you think she will stick with her agreement?"

"I don't know, but if she don't, I know I can count on this family to pull me through it."

They seem satisfied with that. No more questions are asked.

Chapter 11

The dark falls kind of peaceful and just a little arrogant. She is waiting for me, like she knew where I was going tonight. I don't really want to dream. Sometimes I get so weary I just don't even want to dream. The work is fine, but way too intense. I drift off to sleep a piece at a time. Just before I am really sleeping I sit bolt upright and holler, "Buster-Jesus-Christ-second-coming. Who is going to be the Sweat conductor?"

I insulted the Elder who usually performs the Sweats.

"Go to sleep, Will. You'll have a Sweat. You'll have your ceremony. None of these things are dependent on your good behavior, or no one would have showed up to work. You've been reasonably naughty all your life. Now go to sleep," Tony orders.

No dreams come. I am relieved. I awake to the sound of birds singing, dogs barking and the last coyote just howling. I get up. Pop is out there doing Sunrise. God, it has been a long time since I voluntarily opened my eyes this early. Sunrise Ceremony was a summer ceremony in my pop's mind. He is singing his song to the sun. Mom is standing next to him with a copper water container. I fall in beside her. My two brothers straggle in behind me. From out the door and across the yard come Auntie Anne, Lani, Lei-Lani and Callie. I grab my mom's hand. It will likely be the last chance I have to hold it like this.

"I really want to grab your skirt, but I am too tall." Her shoulders shake with laughter, but she makes no sound.

Pop talks to the sun about the changes in this family that are coming down the pipe. He is grateful for them; his pretty wife is tired of mothering and looking forward to playing with grandchildren. He is grateful for himself too. It has been hard for him not to resent these boys who stole time from him in great blocks and positioned themselves like little wedges between he and his beautiful wife. Now they are turning their attention elsewhere, looking out for women of their own.

"Today I give my last son to the world. I don't mind, because Callie has brought me a new son. I hope he is as useful as the ones my wife gave me, because I, too, am weary. Day by day as I become more fragile, I pray you be kind and pave the star path home at the same time as my wife's journey ends."

We join him as he sings and lays out his tobacco.

"Make your way to the river," Pop says to us men. Callie runs back inside, grabs towels and hands them to us.

Callie's husband Richard is with us. My cousin Thomas is inside and my Uncle Thomas pulls up in Eli's car with Eli. My littler cousin Alfred is with them. I don't remember whose son's son he is, maybe it is Eli's daughter's son, he trucks around with Eli and Thomas a lot. The grandkids of these two men are beginning to get old enough to hang out with their grandpas. This family is aging. Well, I guess its always been very new and very old. There has always been grandmas and grandpas, dads, moms, children and every one of them has been a cousin, uncle, or an aunt to someone. I guess I never felt like I was the center of it before.

There is a group of men standing around a secondary fire. They are the shakers, the singers who sang all night for me. Off to one side is my blind granddad. No Buster. I shiver. I miss the days when I used to hang out with granddad and the other old guys, the really old ones.

My granddad is in his nineties. No one knows how old he is. We know he pre-dates white folks in this area except for the Dutch about twenty miles east of here. I spent my boyhood from about age five to ten hanging out with this blind guy, kicking up dust, fishing, wandering the woods and listening to stories every weekend. George and Tony would be with us. If I got tired when I was five, six and seven, one of my brothers would throw me on their shoulders or piggyback me. Who carried them, when they were small? Tony must have carried George and Granddad must have carried Tony, or maybe Tony didn't get carried. The family was pretty thin when Tony was a boy. I remember Tony saying that.

Mom and Pop were shy of brothers and cousins, not like today. Most of us are surviving. I wonder about Pop. Who carried him when he was tired? I am about to slip into one of my reveries when I see Granddad shake his head. He hears me talking and he lifts his finger from his cane to wave me over.

"You stay here—all day and all night. It is the price of manhood." And he leans back and laughs at his own joke.

Eli is the Sweat conductor and Pop's younger cousin George is his helper. Eli has been the firekeeper for Buster for years. I need not have worried.

It is crowded in the Sweat. The dead return in droves. We laugh, we sing, we cry and we talk. Things get resolved in the Sweat for me. I head out of there with both my feet on the ground and the road ahead clear as a bell. The only one who could fog it now is my own foolish and disbelieving self.

After breakfast I go to my room and gather up photos of myself at different ages. I framed them in the frames I had picked up at Zellers months before. I had no idea what I was going to use them for, but now I know. I want to recount my life, to talk about what I know about me, who held me up and who I am grateful to. I also pick up a stone, a crow feather, an eagle claw, and a sprig of cedar and carry the light of the sun, the moon and the stars with me. I am ready. We head for the Longhouse.

Inside the Longhouse fire is burning. Above the fire are the benches, holding my friends and relatives. They are seated and waiting for me to begin. The memory of song, of words and feelings, dances about in my body. I plant my feet on the ground of the house. I am so old and so completely young. I pull up on the fire of the earth underneath my feet and sing my song. I arrange my photos in front of me.

"You have to talk before you giveaway," Eli bellows. The house rocks with laughter.

"Behave yourself Uncle, this is my turn." The house laughs harder, there are whoops of approval and a big, "You go boy," from Eli.

"This first photograph is before my memory begins. You can see someone holding me. Even though I have no memory of being that small, I know those arms. Those arms, cooked, cleaned, combed my hair and the hair of half the people in this house." The drums and sticks roll the beginning of an Eagle Song. I breathe out hard, make that old sound Sto: loh men make, a heavy full sounding "Hau" sound.

"You can't see the head of this woman. I don't believe I saw her head for ten more years after that. She was so invisible to me and so ever present at the same time. She was always ready for whatever disaster I could create, for every need I could conjure, every moment I couldn't seem to get myself involved in, but I didn't really see her. So this photo is fitting. My first memory of the woman who owns these arms is a skirt. Her skirts had deep folds in them. I could hide in them; play coy with my relatives and her friends in them. I could tug at one of the folds like it was a bell-ringer and get fed that way. I could hold onto their folds and be safe in the biggest city... My mom."

The drums roll again—another sound to get me through. "I acknowledge my mom." Then I begin again, "I'm almost five here and that pretty, sweet sixteen-year-old face is another woman who mothered me. She watched out for me when my mom was so tired, it hurt to open her eyes. She hauled me off to school and back again every day for two years. She wore pants, so it was a little more difficult to tug at her, so under her tutelage I actually learned to talk. I acknowledge my sister Callie."

I go over and pick up her son. "This is my first son. In our way, we call our sons by our brothers' names so that their uncles will be reminded that their sisters' sons are their sons, too." Callie stood up, "She named him for me. I acknowledge my first son." Drum roll.

"There I am again. I am swinging on the swing and the woman behind me, pushing me is another woman who mothered me. She still does. She mothered me in the direction of freedom, of choices, of love and joy. I acknowledge my Auntie Josie." As I acknowledge the women, they take a gift out to one of the people. I hold up a picture of me sleeping on Gramma's lap. "We know this picture, don't we, boys. We spent the first five years of our lives on this lap. I can't begin to tell you how grateful I am for that lap. My strength, my resilience, my kindness, my appreciation for just being comes from dreaming in the lap of my gramma." Gramma is crying. Me too. I breathe and fight to find my voice, "I acknowledge my Gramma." I travel through the list of my female relatives one at a time.

"The men here are not finished with me, so I will just say a simple thanks to all you men here who didn't beat the tar out of me even though you really wanted to. I want to thank you for lightening my load when I grew tired. I commit to trying to lighten the load of every generation of Sto: loh men who come after me. Oh, and to the Chief and Council, I do not want to put a belt on and pick up a hammer and saw, but I will, just like all my male relatives... I will. Come Monday, we will begin to build that daycare—government be damned." The drum rolls. I look behind me. My bros George, Thomas, Tony and Richard, Callie's husband, step forward. As I speak, they hand out the rest of the gifts.

"I am moving in the direction of my heritage. Sto: loh men made sure the land was safe. They made sure the territory was bountiful. They took care of this land. I am going to be a caretaker, but a different kind of caretaker than before. I practice my ways. I offer tobacco to the earth, but I think she wants something more. I am going to study to be an environmental scientist, but I plan to do it in a certain way. I want to learn our science first, to ground myself in the science of our holy knowledge, then tailor their science to fit mine. I am going to struggle in an activist way to detoxify this earth, to make this world more responsive to her, to treat her as the beautiful, flexible, fragile and deserving woman she is." Drum roll.

"That's if I can alter the course of my personal history from the guy most likely to ask the dumbest question, to the Sto: loh man who is the caretaker of this island."

The gifts have been given out, my song has been sung and now the food is ready for the feast. Everyone comes to shake my hand.

I'm eating and Lei-Lani is sitting next to me.

"That's about the biggest mouthful of promise I ever heard," she says.

"If you don't think I'm up to it, take a look around, girl. There is a lineup out there for you." It is testy. It is cheeky, but I am full of myself today.

"I wasn't thinking that," she says, "I was thinking how difficult the row you want to hoe is going to be for the woman standing next to you."

Tony looks up from his plate, "He has a lot of kinetic energy, little sister, comes from being the youngest. Everyone's been carrying him for a long time." My brothers laugh again.

"Well, I don't plan to waste any of it," I say.

"What you going to do?" George asks.

"I'm going to spend every weekend I can with Grandpa and his crones. I am going to buy me a computer, get wired to the net. I am going to find me some First Nation scientists. By the time I finish high school I will be on my way to knowing about something."

"I just finished reading a novel by a First Nation woman who wrote about the human genome project and other environmental things. Maybe you could start with her. She seems to know something about us and something about science."

"What's it called?" I raise an eyebrow.

"*Whispering in Shadows*."

"Do you have it here?"

"You borrow books from a library or you buy them from a store, otherwise the author gets cheated of the royalties." I like how Lei-Lani's mind works.

"How did you come to know that?"

"One of my mom's cousins is a writer."

We can see the gentlemen around the table are reasonably impressed with this young woman.

"What I want to know is how does someone as young and pretty as you get interested in knowing something like that," Thomas says looking straight at her.

"You are making me feel bad, sir, about something I have no control over. I inherited these looks. I didn't ask for them or make them up." Lei-Lani says firmly.

Thomas laughs, then apologizes. Lei-Lani finishes eating and gets up to return her plate to the kitchen. I know she likes to play with the water while she is doing dishes, I watched her at mom's house, trailing her fingers through it, probably watching movies in her mind, so she won't be back right away.

"Oooh, she is sweet," Thomas says.

"She just bit your head off."

"And she can do it again," he says.

"She's mine, Thomas. Don't even think about her, it'll break your big old heart."

"She say that to you?"

"She will." I take my plate to the kitchen, but not before handing a challenging look to the men around the table. They wish me luck. I stroll into the kitchen and take hold of her small waist; she turns and smiles. "You mine," I whisper, "when you're ready, you're mine." I squeeze her waist.

"Okay, but you need to spend some time persuading me of that Mister. Don't think just because I agree, I want you to skip any parts of the courtship ritual. You agreed to be a man today, and no one skips over any part of the ritual."

"Fine with me." I go back to the table and swing into my chair in one clean motion.

"She's his, Thomas. I can see it."

"Snooze, you lose," Tony says.

"All he has to do is screw up and I get to catch the fall out. I been doing that for you for years, bro." And they laugh.

This would be true, but I don't plan to screw up. I know it's actually difficult to screw up a relationship with a woman. You have to not care. I cannot see myself not caring. I have had so much caring in my life. I have had buckets full of consideration, devotion and tenderness. All I have to do is pass that on.

A bunch of teenaged girls from Chehalis are walking towards our table. They aren't relatives. I look at Thomas and tell him they're all his and slide out to return to the kitchen. I take to washing pots, doing heavy lifting for the women. If I just hang out with my women relatives for the next four years, I will be okay. Lani says something to her daughter in a language I don't understand, the daughter blushes and keeps washing dishes, her mom gives me that all imperative approving look. I can do this.

Chapter 12

It's Monday. I'm in the cafeteria having lunch. Today after school we meet at the Longhouse, Pop insisted on that. The Chief agreed. I'm a little nervous about it. I know it is going to be a hard row to hoe for the next few days trying to figure out where to begin. No one on this reserve has a backhoe or a bulldozer. A couple of guys have those little BobCat style work mates for small jobs, they will have to do. We have to dig a hole, a big one straight off the top. That means the young guys get to sweat over picks and shovels, while the older guys direct and the two oldest men who can work the BobCats will be busy too. I'm sweating and feeling tired just thinking about it. Some of the women will join us; others will come with food. It's summer so we can work until around 9:00 p.m. before the sunlight fades and if no one collapses. I try hard to remember where the geniuses are going to put the daycare, likely next to the elementary school. Oh man, that field still has trees standing in it. Chainsaws we have.

Wit interrupts my train of thought, "You not hungry or do you just feel like playing with that food. If that's the case, not a good idea, you are a man now I understand."

"Say Wit, Paul, Joseph, sit down." They do. "I just feel like our little nation is in a peck of trouble."

"Are you worried about the daycare, Will? Lei-Lani told me about it." Then Wit looks at Paul and Joseph, "Wasn't all she told me." And he winks. The guys all lean on their chairs. They want to hear the story. I almost want to brag about how easy it was to hook the prettiest Indian woman in the world, but I don't dare.

"She's mine," I say. I believe it. I know it. I don't know why I know it. I just do. I look at them, dead dog serious.

"She's told me you can't have a woman for four more years." Wit says, "That's a long time buddy."

"Lots of doo-doo can happen in four years," Joseph the genuine nerd says.

"Thanks for the confidence guys. But I don't plan to ignore her for the next four years. She already let me know that was not a good idea."

"Good thing too," Thomas says as he swings in across from me, "Because our boy Will, or our man Will, is not known for his insightful brilliance." They laugh.

"But he can fight a battle and win," Paul concedes and gestures to the jocks who are at the end of the room completely ignoring us.

"Give him that," Joseph says.

"What?" Thomas asks.

"That's right. You weren't here. You don't know," Paul tells him in excited language of the day the jocks came to fetch us and I out maneuvered them.

"So that's why they doff their caps to me when I walk by. Here I thought I was just cool."

Some young woman walks towards us. She is one of the jock club's groupies. I say something along those lines to Thomas so he is warned.

"Hi guys," she says all full of flirtation. I don't know what she has up her sleeve, but I don't trust it to be our well-being. The jock groupies come from those well-to-do families who train their girls to please and twist their minds in the direction of manipulation as much as they possibly can. I believe her name is Nancy.

"Whatchaupto?" she says like it is one word.

"Five-foot-nine," I answer, putting my fork down carefully on my plate. "What are you doing here, Nancy?" I ask mustering up the grimmest voice I can.

Nancy is one of the popular girls. She was one of the grade school kids who would say, "Ooh, an Indian," to her buddies every time I passed them, in that disdainful way white girls I've seen do when they believe you are about the most disgusting piece of slime they have ever seen. She must think I have no memory. Besides not liking Indians, she disdains nerds. That about makes this table the last table in the world she wants to stand next to making small talk. I am not sure of what she is up to, but I can guess it ain't good.

"Well. I just thought I would come and say hello, maybe even join you," she sways back and forth.

"Now Nancy. You know this is the nerd table. What could a jock cheerleader want with a bunch of nerds? Now you tell the truth Nancy, just like mommy taught you?"

"I would never call you that."

"To our faces," Wit finishes.

"I don't talk behind your back."

"Nancy. Be nice. Remember my locker is across from yours. I am not deaf and you tend to talk too loud."

"Did you hear?" she asks, terrified. "They made me. They told me they would really hurt me if I didn't do this... I was against it. Honest." She is caught. Sarah was right, neither the jocks nor the nerds mean anything to her.

"If you've been threatened honey, you just sit down and tell Uncle Thomas about it, then we can fix it."

"No, you can't," Nancy cringes.

Thomas is too direct, I'll try another route.

"You're shaking Nancy," I say.

"You would be too, if you were in my shoes."

"Too small," Wit says.

"You know what I am talking about," she scolds.

"For sure I don't," I tell her.

"They'll kill me if I tell."

"Thomas and I won't let them." Thomas raises his eyebrows, then nods. It is enough.

Nancy looks over her shoulders to make sure the jocks are not watching her too closely. She sees they are in their own conversation, laughing and appearing not interested in what Nancy is doing.

"They wanted me to sit with you for a few days, you know, touch you up and stuff, then Friday get you to take me home, then call them and say you tried to... to... to... you know, rape me. They said you wouldn't get hurt, just a bad rep. That I wouldn't have to tell my folks or the cops, just other kids."

They found another avenue. Nancy is afraid of them, at the same time she is also attracted to her source of fear. She is a hostage and although I felt sorry for her, I couldn't let her get away with making me her only prey.

I get up and sashay my way over to the jock table. I have no idea how I look when I walk, but I do know that today all eyes are on me. I hold my chin and try to pull some kind of idea about what I am going to do when I got there.

I figure the jocks are hoping for some raw Siwash rage. Don't give it to them, buddy. I feel my rage come up. I run it through my body like an old lover, put some song, some words to it, then I gather it in the center of my belly like a hot coal, transform it into courage and drop it between my legs. It's there, it isn't going anywhere and now I have endless courage and I can think straight. Sarah's words come back: "Respect Jack." What he has done to this woman is unspeakable. It is his private horror. I am not going to go there, I am going back to before the horror, before his people did things like this to his woman.

"Jack," I say casually.

"Yeah," Jack has a threat in his voice. An insolent so what? He has no idea how stupid it sounds from the other side of his table. There is a guy sitting to my right, slouching easy and relaxed in his chair. I let a bolt of lightning from my coal shoot through my arms, grab the chair, upend it, dump the guy, flip it around and straddle it.

"What the... you see that?" Everyone looks at the floor. The others rise.

"That's right, get up. Now you tell them to take a short walk," I request of Jack and he dismisses them. He looks a little curious about what I plan to do. His buddies don't go far.

"Jack, we going to have a Man Ceremony for you today, just like the one I had Saturday. Today you are going to be a man."

"I don't do that monkey grunting kind of stuff."

"No. What do you call that little game you're playing with your groupie? That is the lowest kind of monkey grunting I ever saw. Now she's your woman, you can do with her what you want, but if you don't let up, you can't be my friend."

He sneers and laughs, "What makes you think I want to be your friend?"

"Because I am smart. I am the kind of guy who becomes a general. I know how to fight and win without shedding any blood. You, you're a sergeant. Now the coach made you the captain because all these monkey-grunters listen to you. They won't listen to me. But you don't know how to win. You can throw that ball, you can kick it, you can catch it, but you can't win. I can win. I can teach you to be a real captain. All you got to do is stick to your bargain."

"And if I don't."

"Your pop's going to get a phone call, explaining why there was no game last Thursday for you."

"What makes you think he'll believe some Indian?"

"He won't, but I am also betting he won't believe you. He'll phone the coach, and the coach he will believe."

There is a pause, tiny beads of sweat form on his forehead.

"Maybe, I told him already," Jack bluffs.

"I know what you told him, because you talk in the shower to your monkey-grunting cronies. I know your phone number because two years ago you passed me a note for Nancy in class. On the outside was a number. In the hallway that afternoon Nancy was bragging to her girlfriends that you passed her your phone number. Now a sergeant doesn't pay attention to that, but a general does. I have always known that if I am going to have any trouble in this institution that it was going to come from your corner."

"And if I do become your friend?"

"You are going to be the captain of the best football team in this province. From high school to university college takes more than grunt work. You have to get your grades up in the next two years so you can play on a university team; otherwise no pro football team is going to see you. You know how important it is for you to play pro football."

"What do I got to do?"

"Back off. I'll be your friend, before and after the game. Now I am going to jump up and tell everybody in this room that we had some misunderstanding but we sat down and talked it out like men and now we are friends. You get up behind and say as much."

I stand up. "Everybody! Pay attention. Jack and I have had some words. Those words were misunderstood, but we had a chat and now we see our way clear to a lasting friendship. We apologize to everyone in the room if we caused any discomfort."

Jack is standing beside me, nodding his head, his body slouching and his one leg shaking. He can hardly breathe.

It's his turn. He doesn't look up. I whisper "breathe" to him, tell him he's bigger, he can do it. He smiles a little and lifts his head.

"I, I just want to say, the misunderstanding is over and we're friends now me and da Chief." Sarah's table stifles a laugh. Jack sits down.

"Meet me ten minutes before the game." I tap him on the shoulder a couple of times and leave. His buddies return. They talk. Jack is trying to tell them the gist of what I said. He looks frustrated. I hear the conversation as I slowly make my way across the room.

"You had to be there. If we back off, we get to win at football," Jack affirms.

"How do you know?" another jock asks.

"Well, we will know first game Ike, won't we?" Jack says.

"Yeah. Guess you're right."

Halfway to my table Nancy hurries by. I grab her by the waist before she gets away. "Nancy," I whisper, "Where you going in such a hurry. You threatened me and I can't let you get away with that." I swing her around beside me and walk her back to my table. The jocks are watching.

"I didn't threaten you. I wouldn't threaten anyone." She believes herself.

"You don't think planning to call me a rapist to these good people here is a threat?"

"They... " I cut her off the pass.

"You were going to see it through, now you are going to take it back. You are going to tell these people, that if you ever say anything bad about me it is because someone threatened you."

"I don't have to say sorry."

"No. You don't have to say sorry, just tell the truth."

"I don't have to say who put me up to it."

"No."

"Everybody, can I have your attention, please. Go on Nancy," I put my hand on the small of her back and whisper, "Breathe."

"I just want to say that I would never say anything bad about Will." The tears are falling; her voice is breaking. I whisper, "Breathe," again. I tell her that she is a good woman. She regains her voice, "If you hear me say anything bad, it's because somebody threatened me into it." She tries to run. I grab her and hold her. She is sobbing. I walk her out of the cafeteria. In the hall I ask her how come she is with someone who demeans her like this, who threatens her into doing things she would not do on her own? A man should make a free woman of you. When she is finished crying she says sorry for messing up my shirt. I tell her it's okay and advise her to see the school counsellor. She lets go a winsome "yeah" and walks to the bathroom a little wobbly on those high platform shoes of hers.

"I seem to be bothering everybody today, but I want your attention one more time. I have been mistreated by almost everyone in this room from grade school up. I will be sixteen tomorrow. Today is the last day I put up with any abuse. I just want to get along, enjoy my friends and get through three more years. Don't give me a hard time."

I sit down and lean back in my chair feeling like a crazy

combination of Denzel Washington, Sidney Poitier and Chief Dan George. I want to grin from ear to ear. Today, they don't like me any better, but they will respect me.

"So. Denzel is it now," Wit asks. I smile. "You certainly are solving problems and putting out fires today."

"The biggest one is coming tonight," I say.

"Daycare?"

"Yeah, complex is more like it."

"What's daycare?" Joseph asks. Wit tells me to explain. I do. Joseph is frowning.

"So your only real problem is no one can read the plans and translate that into action. You don't have a site supervisor." Joseph pulls out his cell phone. I can't believe he has one. I mention it to the table that I didn't know he had one. Someone mentions that we have only been friends for five days; five days by the way, that has been filled with more excitement and problems than either of them has seen in their lifetime. We laugh.

I hear Joseph on his cell saying, "Hi Dad," but then he gets up from the table and turns his head moving the cell around as if looking for better reception. After a few minutes he hangs up and sits back down.

"If you feed him. My dad will show one of you how to read plans and do site supervision from six to nine every night for a week, then once a week after that."

"How much?"

"Well he likes recognition. I bet he'd like the idea of being Potlatched, honoured by a First Nation and he is quite crazy about your art. A feast and an art piece ought to do it, though he says he will do it out of the goodness of his heart and because he knows we didn't have to pay a dime for this country. My dad is a liberal."

"Let me use your cell, Joseph." I phone my Chief. He gets excited. I don't believe I have ever heard our Chief get excited.

"I am going to be a hero after this," I say, "I just saved my Chief's bacon. He says he owes me. I believe I have a summer job from now till I get my Masters." That stills the table.

"I didn't know you were planning on going on to university, Will," Joseph says and the others agree by nodding their heads, with murmers of "Yeah."

"Why wouldn't I?"

"No reason, 'cept most Natives don't. Look around; Sarah is the only one in her twelfth year out of ten that started out in eighth grade. You, Thomas, Lila and Wit, who is barely Native, are all that's left of the ninth graders and you are it for tenth grade." Joseph points directly at me.

"You serious about finishing?" Paul asks.

"We were all serious about finishing when we started here, Paul, but look at the hoops I have had to jump through over the past week just to be able to sit down and *eat* and *play* a game of football without getting injured by my teammates. You think it's like this at home for me? After a while, carving, shake-splitting and fishing begins to look good."

"I know," Paul says, "You're preaching to the choir. We were here. We saw it. Hell, I had more trouble in the last three days than the rest of my school life and I am a nerd. I know."

"What he is trying to tell you is we have a study group if you boys care to join. It is how we raise our individual grade points. We meet on Friday," Joseph finishes.

"I believe I would like to join. What about you, Thomas?"

Thomas says, "Yeah," and we are in. Thomas has dreams; dreams of going to medical school, but neither of us have a clue how to raise his grade points. They aren't that low. He is nowhere near flunking, but med school takes near perfect grades in high school. It is all Thomas ever wanted to be. He gets excited.

"What about the daycare?" Wit asks.

"They can have me every day but Friday," Thomas says it without hesitation. I like that about him. Once he has a goal he stays with it come hell or high water till he realizes it.

"Every day but Friday," I repeat and we laugh.

Chapter 13

On the way home Thomas says to me, "Will, I do believe we have some friends."

"Yeah," I say, "These are our first friends, aren't they, Thomas? Everyone else in our life has been family, but these guys, these guys are friends."

"Yessiree-Bob. We have entered the new millennia," he says breaking into a song, "I got friends in low places, where the whiskey's fine..." and we are rolling down the Rez road singing Garth Brooks at the top of our lungs.

We arrive at the Band Hall after supper. The Chief is talking to Joseph's father. Joseph is hanging out. There are a couple of our best carpenters there, along with Pop and Uncle Eli. I am not sure why they are there, but we are all waiting until some game plan is arrived at. No one is calling this meeting to order or letting anyone know when things will get started. I have some angst about this part of the way we all are.

I know the maxim: "Patience. The tide will roll in, the rain will fall, the sun will rise, blah, blah, blah, but humans have language, and they could let us know we would be assembling in fifteen minutes. That way we would have some sort of idea of how long we will have to wait. We could all be doing something that is mildly interesting besides waiting. We know it takes fifteen minutes to stroll outside, have a smoke, tell a few jokes, or get ourselves a coffee and go to the bathroom. This way, we aren't sitting thinking any minute, any minute, any day now, come on guys, any day now. I decide to duck outside.

Joseph joins me along with Thomas, George and some of our cousins. Tony rolls in with Rachel in tow. The women need to be here to figure out what their role is in relation to all this. We know they will need to do something. They will figure out what they are prepared to do once they hear the work plan, the grocery list of things to do. They will tell us and then we shall carve up the rest amongst ourselves.

"Some of the women are carpenters?" Joseph asks.

Thomas and the others crack up. "You on the *Rez* now, boy. These gals can do anything, better'n half of us."

Joseph has no idea what it's like here. He is a little miffed. I shoot Thomas a look and tell him in the language that Joseph does not have to be here, we do. Thomas shuffles.

"So, I should treat him like a woman," he says in the language.

"No, you should behave like a guest toward him."

"Same thing," he says in English. You technically cannot be a man's guest inside a house. You could be a guest on his boat, or in the bush, so I mention that. Thomas thinks that that is so completely different from what I am asking. I mean on another man's boat, you would be using his tools, or in his bush you would be shooting the deer he knows, his relatives.

"What do you suppose the ability to read plans is, bro?" This comes from George, "Laundry?" Thomas gets it.

"Sorry, man. I am just naturally a persnickety guy, if you catch my drift." Not much of an apology, but it is the best Thomas can do. Joseph has already gotten over what Thomas had said and so looks a little confused. We can't resist laughing. We backtrack for him.

"Is there anything I should know about conduct?" Joseph asks.

This is one of the hardest questions to answer. You want to say don't be your usual self, because usually you people are invasive. But it is a cultural thing for them, like the question about the women being there. We have rules, but whether or not you follow them is a matter of integrity. It is not like men and women usually do things together, but it is not like we don't either, likewise with them. They will have women on the site standing next to a coffee wagon or bringing food, but this is not the women's clear choice. The men plan, then deploy, they call on you depending on what they believe you can do, and not coordinate you based on what you choose to do. So how do we answer a question that comes at life and all its manifestations from such really different directions?

"We begin life without language—just our eyes and ears. Spend some time learning about our life," Tony offers. Good one.

"Listen and watch... I can do that."

"Because he is just that talented," Thomas offers.

A good hour has gone by, with us just waiting outside the Band Hall. We are all beginning to get antsy. Joseph too. He really wants to say something, but he was told to listen and watch. Simple instructions, but hard to manage.

They are calling us in. They have a plan. The Chief names all the people in charge, tells us what they are in charge of, lets us know that those without demonstrable skills are to attach ourselves to someone with skills. They run through the list of men who have demonstrable skills, name the skills, name who is coordinating the kind of work they are doing and ultimately who is in charge of sections of the project. Mr. Williams, Joseph's dad, is our overseer. I have no demonstrable skills; I hook onto Tony who has some, along with Thomas. Joseph asks if it is all right to hook up with us. We look at him. We obviously weren't in the same meeting hall. Tony repeats everything the Chief just said almost word for word, then stares at him.

"No one threw you out of the hall, boy. That means those words were for you." He decides to hook up with us. "Here, there is choice in the narrowest context of freedom," I tell him.

He has all kinds of misgivings, questions about; what if there is too many of us all in one heap? Maybe we should split up? What if we do the wrong thing? He has no way of knowing that here it doesn't matter. If we are asked to split up, we will, no problem. It only means something to people who are constantly being examined. I think the tests at school give these people an inordinate amount of insecurity because they take it so seriously—it is really how they are *siem*. They do not want to do the wrong thing. Here it doesn't matter. We are all doing the wrong thing. Not one of us has a clue what we are doing. We are undertaking the construction of a major complex without any papered carpenters, electricians, and plumbers and with only vague notions of landscaping, drainage and blueprint reading. This is so completely wrong. Most of us have never swung a hammer and those that have built sheds, porches, at best additions. This is so wrong. We all ought to have our heads examined.

I find a spare belt in Pop's truck and hand it to Joseph. Thomas hands him a hammer and a saw. He looks at the saw. It is a nice one: a wormdrive. I have a small circular Black & Decker. I trade Joseph for it. He is pretty grateful. A worm is a pretty heavy little beast. Pop comes over.

"Could you boys start cutting 2 x 4s? Use rough lumber only. There is a bunch of second hand lumber over there. Make sure there is no nails in it."

"Six feet long?" Tony asks.

"Yeah. It's just for forming the basement," Pop says and leaves. Tony has Joseph removing nails. Thomas and I cut and Tony sorts out the wood.

Pop comes back. Here it comes. He is going to ask us to dig. I wish I was not one of the six biggest guys on this Rez. There is no hesitation in Pop's walk. He has never experienced any reluctance from either of us. We have never expressed any. I won't start now. I notice there is someone walking behind him. It is Rachel and Sarah. They take our saws and hammers from us with a sweet smile each. Joseph looks at Tony, but says nothing, just watches us walk away.

"It is 7:30 p.m. Good, only an hour and a half left of daylight," I say, but Thomas points at a pair of guys setting up the bleacher lights.

"Oh Jesus," I sigh.

Pop comes by and announces, "10:00 p.m. is quitting time. Shall we make some progress boys?" He drops a wheelbarrow and leaves. Not long after that Josie comes by with a wagon of sandwiches and coffee in a number of Thermos bottles. She gives us a Thermos and a lunch bag.

Pop is heading this way with Joseph in tow. Joseph no longer has a saw. He will be pushing the wheelbarrow. I'm eating a sandwich and sipping on a coffee. Pop frowns. Josie hands Pop a bag. He tucks it in his shirt. I think about tucking my bag in my shirt, then decline. I am hungry. Pop shifts his shoulders and loses the frown. Thomas has the barrow full and I am finished my sandwich. Most of the people moving the wheelbarrows are women and smaller teenaged boys.

I decide that digging is idiot's work. There is a string marking the cut line. We cut, then dig. Pop drops a stick by that will mark how deep. There is a pickaxe in case we need it. There is a pair of BobCats digging out the center and moving it to the pile of excess dirt. We are getting down to sand and gravel, good for building, bad for digging. Thomas starts swinging a pick. I hum an old paddle song. Thomas picks up the rhythm. The guys next to us call it back. Pretty soon we are all singing, every now and then Pop lets go a 'whoomph' kind of sound, the old guys join him about every two bars of call back and forth. It makes the work easier.

My grandpa and a few other disabled Elders arrive with their drums. They are too old to work but they can sing us through it. I see my mom drive up with Pop's truck. She has a load of old wood. Suzy and Jay are unloading, their babies are in the truck with Mom. They are unloading next to Tony, who is talking to Pop. Wait a minute. There must not be enough money even for materials. I close my eyes. I do not want to look and see my tired mom unloading that lumber. I do not want to think about her fifty-year-old body having to put her back to this plough after her last son has gone and entered manhood. Thomas is staring.

"It ain't right," he says. He marches over there. Pop tells him to go back to where he put him. He bites his lip, but then hollers, "It ain't right, not Auntie Mary." I know that hurt Pop, he comes over.

"We need more than we got here Thomas, you can see that. She set her mind to unloading and loading. Go with it." Thomas breathed out hard, big sound and big breath. I look up and see my mom laughing and unloading, but I feel like Thomas.

"When does it end Pop? When do we say enough with these guys?"

"Dig," was all he said. Thomas dug harder and faster. So did I. I was sorry about my hesitation earlier. If we don't do this, the women will. Pop knew that. The best he could do was making sure the heaviest work was done by the most able. I could feel Grandpa's sweat oozing pain, oozing love. Pop somewhere along the line just accepted all this. I look out and realize over half the village is here. Some of the kids pushing barrows of stone, sand and gravel are just kids. One barrow has two kids at the end of it. Damn we are pathetic. Thomas stops looking. I am glad cause I look up and I see Auntie digging. Thomas will have a fit if he sees that. I recall Sarah's words, "Don't take it too seriously. If you do, you will want to kill somebody."

Grandpa has another song going. Thomas seriously digs and I do too. I take the time out to join the song. Pretty soon Thomas does too. Some of the words to this one are funny. It's set up like a stand-up comedy joke complete with a punch line, but it only works in the language. We start to enjoy the madness. It is funny. Here we are in the year 2000 digging a hole with pick axes and shovels. These guys can get each other to the moon but they can't get us a daycare.

Grandpa's memory pops up, "There was a quiet time in this village before you were born. We just stayed in our houses, didn't seem to have the energy to do anything. We seemed to stop breathing. Then some young city boys started pushing back. It woke us up. We just woke up one day, took a look around and decided to do something for ourselves. We have been clipping along pretty good since then." Grandpa laughed after he told me this. Like it was so ridiculous to ever have fallen asleep like that. There are some jokes that you have to live through to get. He tried to explain it to me, but it didn't stick.

10:00 p.m. quitting time. A whistle blows. People start leaving the field. Joseph looks like he is going to faint.

"How are you getting home, Joseph?" Thomas sounds genuinely concerned. Somehow Joseph had kept up with our rage driven furious digging. He earned himself a ton of respect. He half smiled at Thomas. He felt the tenderness in the words.

"Don't worry. My dad is still here."

"We might as well hang out till you leave. If I know my pop, we will be the last to go."

"You want to work till then?" Joseph asks.

"Are you kidding?" I reply with a little too much intensity.

Joseph laughs. He caught us. It was his first crack at an Indian joke. He nailed us.

We get home around 11:00 p.m. I am so tired I forget that my room is free and head for the tent. It isn't there. George comes out. "Your bed is upstairs, Will."

"Oh yeah," I stagger up the stairs and flop on the bed without removing my clothes.

Chapter 14

Animals are everywhere. Crazy old foxes building dens, prairie chickens hauling twigs for nests, dodging the foxes, fish jumping getting ready for the journey home, heading for the last spawning moment of joy to die in the river in the same spot they were born in. I am first a fox, then the chicken, then the salmon. The walls of canyons appear. In the faces of the canyons are faces of the animals, they change to my relatives, then back to animals, the stone walls have seeds tucked inside them. These seeds cry out. They burst through the stone, and flowers bloom on the canyon wall. I can hear the pain of birth everywhere. I'm digging mindlessly, hopelessly, digging at the canyon wall, picking at its rock face, feeling more fragile than the flower seeds that push their way through stone. My body heats up; the sun is raking my skin and it's time to wake up.

The kitchen is near deserted. Aunt Josie is there but not my mom, my pop or George.

"Where is everybody?"

"At the daycare," Josie says and laughs her lusty laugh. She is laughing because we are all calling it a daycare and it is barely a hole in the ground. "That is one of the many differences between us and white people," she says, "They call it what it is, a construction site, a daycare site or just a site, not us. We have decided it will be a daycare so daycare it is. Have some coffee and some of my pie, Will. You don't like this work, do you?"

"Does it show?" I wait for her laugh. It doesn't come.

"Yeah," she says, kind of melancholy, like she wished I did like it.

"I can't Auntie. I tried looking at it every which way. It's digging. It's grunt work. It's idiot's work."

"Most of life is," she says softly, "You get up in the morning, you Chit, Chower and Chave, then you eat, you wash dishes, you drive to work. It all starts out interesting when it's new. Soon as you know what you're doing it becomes grunt work, idiots work, just plain old digging. Doctors dig around in bodies, carpenters dig in a tool box, women dig around in the sink, babies dig around in the mud..."

"What do scientists dig around in Auntie?"

"Concepts." My turn to laugh. Aunt Josie has some point of view.

"Well now, I have nothing interesting to look forward too."

"Don't be so lazy," she says, rolling a cigarette.

"What?"

"Make it interesting."

"How?"

"Now how would I know how to make things interesting for you? I have no idea how your insides work. Me, I dig around in food. I tell myself all kinds of nonsense about food. Cake is girlie, no cake for boys. Pies are for boys, they are round and substantial, cake is fluffy and sweet. It's all fiction honey, but it makes the same old, same old interesting. You stop telling yourself stories you can't live anymore. You don't learn to story up the mundane, and love that, you can never be happy. I get bored enough; I start turning food into characters, get them telling stories themselves."

I am sitting on the counter. Aunt Josie has a carrot and an onion. The carrot is talking to the onion, bragging about how sweet she is, while the onion tells her he is substantial. I am laughing like crazy. The carrot dances around in a circle.

"Look at my pretty coloured orange. I am like fire," she is using a high-pitched girls voice and a slightly different Salish accent.

"Oh yeah, well purple is the colour of independence, it's what makes me substantial," says the onion in a deep baritone." He rolls. Not all that surprising, but certainly not as pretty as the carrot.

"Make them fight. Make them fight," I say getting excited.

"Now, now, Willie, that would be playing with the food," she says laying down the carrot and picking up a fork, making it bob back and forth in a mock scolding tone. We both laugh which means the game is over.

"Carrots, Willie, is girl's food. Onions are for boys and garlic is for everyone."

All this time I thought Josie's maxims were serious understandings about our cultural relationship to food. I thought she was entertaining me, but she was just bored. "I get it Auntie," and I laugh at the memory. That's it, I say to myself, Aunt Josie is never bored.

"Do you sew, Josie?"

She shows me her hands. They are all knotted up. It looks like rheumatoid arthritis. I guess I never noticed before.

"When did that happen?"

"Years ago at Residential School. I think I was your age."

"They did that to you?"

"I think so. Not like they tortured me or anything, just fed me their food in small amounts. I was about your age when it happened. That summer, your gramma took a look at my hands and she never sent me back. All I remember after that is missing the gals. Three hundred days a year with the same gals, year after year. I spent more time with them than this family until then. It took me until I was twenty-five to catch up. At first, I hung about the outer edges of your mom's life, then Gramma, my gramma, your great gramma says, "You got to participate in your own life, or you will die inside, get in there. My twisted little hands couldn't sew after that, but I could cook, tell a passable story and I could learn to enjoy my family. It took me twenty-five years to catch up, but I did. Will, the only time I was bored is when I didn't bother to participate in my life."

I want to stop the story. It was choking, sucking up the air in the room, halting the thoughts inside my mind, and spilling ice slivers into my blood. I did not need to know this about that place. I had heard about the abuses, the beatings, the hunger and the rapes, but this made the whole thing a horror story. I know my pop never went, but Mom did, for twelve long years. I begin to re-look at her life here in this community, in this family, her loyalty to us. A purple veil of understanding starts rising and the ice slivers in my blood melt. Mom works, like Great Grandma did, like a workhorse, but she rarely enjoys her life. I don't know how it is with Pop in the privacy of their bedroom. It must be okay, but then Pop's words come, "The kids came and I kind of disappeared."

"You ever talk like this to Mom?"

"About playing with food. Are you nuts?"

"No. About learning to enjoy the family again."

"No," she said looking at me strangely, "You do pick up on the strangest side of a sentence Will. Thomas is here, you better go to school." She hands me a lunch bag and just looks at me while I leave. Thomas is at the door when I get there, shoulder hunched.

"What's up?"

"You want to go down by the river?"

"Sure." I know better than to ask why. It doesn't matter. Something is really bothering Thomas. He wouldn't interrupt his schooling for illness, so to detour this morning and risk missing the bus, this must be important. I hope no one died. He has his hands in his pockets all the way there. At the river he takes his left hand out holds it against his chest. He means to talk to the woman in the river: Warrior Woman some call her, Salmon Woman to others. She is the woman who takes care of the salmon run and so in a sense she is the auntie to us, if the earth be the mom that is, and she takes care of us.

"Help us make this daycare," he ends and carefully lays the tobacco out on the water. We watch the flakes of tobacco slowly join a rapid, then they join a bigger one, finally the tobacco gets roiled at the center of the river a flake at a time, until it all disappears. We head for the bus. We cross

Morrow's field, hoping to cut the bus off at the pass. It has to wind its way around the farms and the river. We get to edge of the corn rows and there comes the bus, bumping around the last curve. It stops. We swing in next to Sarah.

"Where were you guys?" I stare at her. She is hissing like she is one of my aunties. Sarah is already a grown-up Sto: loh woman.

"Down by the river offering tobacco for the daycare," Thomas answers. "We need this thing to happen. I have no idea why, but I dreamed it last night. Great Grandpa was there in my dream. I was telling him that we need it to happen and he was agreeing. So I thought I better offer tobacco."

Sarah and I make the sound everyone makes in the big house when they are hearing words they know are so profoundly true that it rocks the senses, that someone could just come up with them like that and somehow find the good sense to know that someone else needed to hear it. People don't always listen to themselves, hear the significance in their words, but every now and then, someone hears themselves say something serious and they recognize it. We stroke the person with that sound to encourage him to go on recognizing the significant things they're saying, not to compliment the thought. Thinking is a given, recognizing important thoughts is a gift.

The bus passengers are so quiet today. We worked the giggles and the gaggles out of us last night. Everyone on this bus was at the site, digging till 10:00 p.m.

"Hey, everybody, three strokes on the head and three pats on the back for all that digging," Sarah hollers out. We all whoop and cheer for ourselves. This brings back the chatter and the chuckles and I relax a little, surprised at how tense I was and even more surprised that I only noticed after the fact. Why is that?

• • • •

It's a game day. I arrive ten minutes early. Jack is sitting in the locker room waiting.

"Playing a game isn't about just skill, Jack. It's about relaxation and concentration, first you got to learn to relax." My Grandpa's words come easily. Grandpa wasn't talking about football, he was talking about *Lahal* when he gave me that advice. But that same advice works for most every game.

"Breathe deep, down to your butt, make your whole torso expand." I show him from the side. Ask him if he can see my butt expand.

"Are you nuts? Don't play with me, man." He gets up turns and looks away.

"Whose MVP here, you or me? Do as I say," I tell him.

"Well, I'm the captain of the team," he says in his defence.

"Just answer the question Jack, whose MVP?"

"You."

"Then do as I say." He tries it, fails. I am looking at him. I could not get through a game breathing as shallow is this big guy does. It is the first time I realize how truly large this boy is. He stands six foot four at least and weighs out at 190 pounds. Compared to him, I'm a peewee. It's awesome to think about the potential this guy has as a breathing player. First I get him gathering up his tension into a ball and blowing it out, then get him to try breathing again. He needs to make the sound. I get him to try it. He does. Finally, he breathes well and deep then lets it go, coughing all the way out.

"Go get a drink of water, you're toxic."

"Toxic?"

He comes back. We practise breathing again, first making the sound, then hauling in air and letting her go real slow. He manages three clean slow breaths. He is standing straight up now, not his usual slouch. I would mention this but he would not likely appreciate it, slouching is cool. Sometimes these people confuse: if it's bad for you, it's cool. I ask him how he feels.

"Light-headed," he says.

"You'll get used to it. Did it ever occur to you your head shouldn't feel that heavy." He cracks up. Then gets quiet. He is shuffling a little.

"Hey, man. All those time in practice when we hurt ya... no hard feelings." He is whispering now.

"Sure. Now, Jack, just before you run out on the field not just at the beginning of a game, but every time—do the breath work."

"Is that why you do that?"

"Yeah. Look at me. I am a little guy compared to you. I have to do something to keep from getting killed out there. Enough for today. Next game, ten minutes early."

"I always wondered how you held your own out there," he says and I laugh. Soon we are all getting into uniform. Jack actually looks relaxed; he is standing up straight looking like some giant compared to the rest of us. Jack is a super player, but he was never able to hold out for much of the game. His breath was too shallow and he was too tense. Except for me, he has been injured more times than the rest of the team put together.

This time Jack's breathing seems to help his game. He holds out and we win. The guys are rubbing his head and patting his back. He just smiles at me and shakes his head. You never know, with some oxygen in his brain, he may learn to think too.

I am wandering out of the building when I catch my mom coming out of the stands. No one in my family watches our sports games. That used to make me kind of sad, but it doesn't anymore. It isn't any meanness on their part; it just doesn't seem relevant to them. They view school as a tool. It seems like, for white people, attending the game reflects the school spirit of the parents. To my folks that would be like cheering on a chainsaw. It doesn't make sense to them.

"I had to pick you up, so I thought I would catch a game of this football stuff." She busts up laughing, "You all look so funny, dressed like that."

I laugh too. I used to think that we looked pretty silly too; all that padding and helmets.

"What is the point of the game?"

I try to explain it to her. She can't stop laughing and running over some of the more hilarious plays, a dozen guys just grabbing, pulling, running and pushing each other.

"Looked like a bunch of human crash up derby cars," and she laughs some more, "You like that game, son?"

"Well since you put it that way, I am half afraid to admit that I do."

"Oh, I am sorry. I just can't help it."

"How is it at the daycare?"

"The daycare? It's starting to look like a hole. Those little BobCats can do a lot of work." Poor Mom, she is impressed with so little progress.

"I was talking to Aunt Josie this morning." Where did that come from? It seemed to drop out of my mouth all by itself. Momma pulls up to Tim Hortons on the way out of town. We park but don't get out.

"Yeah, Aunt Josie told me." She sits there for a minute clutching the steering wheel so hard her hands turn almost white.

"I never thought I would have to talk about this. Residential School. I was so angry in that place, son. Every day I was angry. It wore me out. I just can't get mad over it anymore. At least that was what I thought. I kept journals in there, hid them between the mattresses of my bed. I took them home every holiday, that someone sent for me—not many times; no money; not many at all; two summers and three times for Christmas. Josie and I talked all day about it as we dug out that daycare. By the end of the day, I was furious again. I told Josie about the journals."

Mom pauses, then begins to tell me about her and Josie's conversation, "Josie asked me if I still had those old journals. She put her gnarled little fingers up to her face the way she does, hiding her crippled little hands. I went and got the journals to show her. Then when Josie lit up a smoke, leaned back in her chair, her head tossed to one side, showing that magnificent angle to her face, tears started rolling down my face. They crippled her, honey and I couldn't get up the caring between us to feel that."

Her shoulders shake. She is crying. I reach over and put my hand on her shoulder. My body gets really quiet.

"Imagine that, I just couldn't feel for my own sister. No sewing. Imagine a life with no sewing... I felt for her for the first time today."

She picks up the bag and hands it to me. Inside are some tattered little scribblers. I stare at them. My mom's childhood is in these pages.

"I don't know why I want to give them to you, but here they are. Maybe you can figure something out from them. Me, I am still too angry about it all to figure out what to do."

"Thanks," I finger the books trying hard to feel grateful.

"No thanks to you, son. I think I didn't truly love my little sister until today." Mom wipes her eyes and clears her throat, "Now let's get some of that old Tim Hortons." I slip the books back into the bag and head into Tim Hortons, holding the door open for my mom.

In lineup some guy in front of us is joking, all friendly, with my mom. He is about her age. I wonder if he lived here back in those Residential School days. Looks like it; coveralls, a plaid shirt, farm clothes. I bet he never once gave it a thought that he lived next door to a thousand Sto: loh and never saw one of them in his school. Probably just thought we were too dumb to send our kids to their schools.

"You from here?" I ask him. Mom shoots her foot back to step on mine.

"Yeah. Born and bred." Mom's foot dances on mine and she leans in to my shoulder to warn me. She whispers, "Be careful, son. I don't know what you are thinking, but that is Tommy's grandson. Tommy and his family have always done right by us." We grab our coffee and go.

We are late arriving to the daycare. All the kids have been working for an hour or more. Josie is milling among all the busy people with her wagon of sandwiches, talking all sexy and sultry to everyone. She teases this one, then that one, encouraging everyone. She plays a little with the younger ones, making her life interesting for herself. I like that. Mom's right, there is a tilt of her head that is pure magic. She does it a lot. I tilt my head like that. It does feel good, not arrogant, but cheeky. I grab a shovel and swing in next to Thomas. Pop comes over and takes a kid who is pushing himself to try to keep up with Thomas and has him start pulling nails out of second-hand plywood instead. Mom watches me for a minute getting to work then jumps back in the truck and drives off.

I think she's must be heading for Tommy Morrow's place. She's probably thinking, maybe he has some lumber; maybe his friends have some.

When Mom gets back she tells me that over coffee with Tommy, he made a few phone calls to some of the local farmers he knows to see if they have clean lumber left over from building projects. On Mom's behalf, he asked a farmer, who is the owner of a hardware store, if we can have the lumber.

"As long as you're going to tear it down and haul it your-selves?" Tommy had repeated from the phone to Mom, and Mom gave him a "yes" nod.

The hardware store owner wanted to make sure Tommy was going to be there too. Tommy agreed and told Mom, "I'm sorry," he said, "I have be there with you."

Mom laughed and told Tommy, "You are a funny man. He makes you eat up a weekend on a bunch of Indians and you're apologizing to me. I like your company, so don't say sorry to me." Then Mom asked him, "You don't mind do you, Tommy?" He said he didn't mind at all.

After Mom tells me this she shows me the back of the truck, full of lots of clean lumber. This changes things. The foreman wants to begin seriously tackling a corner so they can start the forming. It isn't what the site supervisor had said to do, but we go ahead. We crowd down one end, men and BobCats, and in an hour there is a space ready for forming.

Two little guys, around seven-years-old, show up about an hour after we start. Each little guy has a handle on a wheelbarrow and they're grunting and shoving trying to get some kind of rhythm going to their movement. I think they must have seen the bigger guys heave and move with steady rhythm the barrows of dirt and were trying to get the hang of it. By eight thirty that evening when their mothers came to get them, the boys were doing pretty good. On the one hand, I was proud of the boys, the girls, and the women and on the other, sick to my stomach that we all had to get out there, because the government had dragged its feet and cost the Band in architectural overruns. Everything we try to do seems to end in the same morass as the mud-stuck-road

building of the turn of the century. I pictured them building with not enough gravel, Jimmy constantly complaining
and Great Grandpa and Great Grandma, the Tsimpsians,
the Asian Charlie and the non-English speaking boys from
Spuzzum, all having to figure out how to solve the problem
with whatever nature had at hand. Almost a hundred years
have passed and nothing seems to have really changed.

I quit thinking about it. We slide along the outside of the
building, BobCats and men, wheelbarrows and children digging a trench and hauling dirt. The formers are right behind
us, shaping the walls at the edge of the would-be building.
We very nearly get her shaped in a night.

Chapter 15

I swing into my seat at what had become our table. Lunch with the guys is different today. Joseph had worked till 10:00 p.m. with his dad at the site. Likely, he had never done so much physical labour in his entire life. I chuckle about it as I try to see it from Joseph's point of view. A scraggly herd of turtles, without hard hats or real modern gear trying to move a mountain and construct a modern building with only crude tools. Kids, women, men, teenagers and three white guys; Joseph is one, his father is another, and the ever-ready Tommy Morrow. I wonder if he was as horrified as I was at the notion of my mother and Tommy scavenging second-hand lumber and my sisters and girl cousins pulling nails while the builders scoured the de-nailed mess for decent pieces to build forms.

Jack is approaching. I am not in the mood for this kind of trouble. He sits across from me. Out of the corner of my eye I see Joseph, Paul and Wit standing at the end of the cafeteria line and hesitating. They aren't in the mood either. I nod for them to come on over, then look at Jack.

"Good game huh?" He says. *Good start Jack; at least it wasn't adversarial.* "Treat him with respect," Sarah had said.

"You were awesome," I tell him. It was the truth. He seems to be more clear-headed and aggressive in a productive way; more confident, like his belief in himself had been born. The smile on his face was like a kid's grin; the one kids get when they win at darts at a carnival, humble and proud at the same time. Humans are much more beautiful if the emotions they are putting out are layered or paradoxical. Next time I am going to teach him about anger worn as a mask and moved by an old sly fox attitude.

"Yeah, thanks," he says. The nerds have arrived. They stare at Jack.

"Excuse me. I just wanted to say hello to Will." Jack rises, not ready to join my friends, but definitely not pugilistic—another win.

"Take it easy, man," I hail him off.

"From nerds to jocks, that is quite a pendulum swing," Joseph says, "You must be quite the diplomat." He sits carefully.

"From technoweenie to mud humper, that's quite a pendulum swing," I reply, "You must be quite the human being." We both laugh.

Thomas asks how he feels in the softest voice he can muster. Joseph says we do not want to go there. "I have muscles that are aching that God did not seriously intend man to use." We crack up. He tells his version of the day-care construction.

"Little bitty babies were wheeling dirt better than me." He schlepps his fork on to the table with great mock indignation. "Old ladies worked harder than me." I look down at the table. He stops me from falling in a major pity party.

"Quit feeling sorry for yourselves. Just once, just once, take some pride in doing something no white community could possible do," he says with fierce determination. "With no money, you are building a very fine complex, a daycare, a high school and a senior's center, which by the way is going to operate as a single unit. You can feel sorry for yourself when you are old and the way things are have changed. In the meantime just feel good about what you have." Thomas looks askance at Joseph.

"Why Joseph, I think a little Sto: loh must have jumped in your jeans last night, 'cuz you sound just like Grandpa." He cracks up. This tells me Thomas has found a way out of his moroseness. He truly hates to be morose. I throw in the towel.

"Okay, Joseph, sir." I realize this is Joseph's finest hour. He is truly feeling proud of himself for the first time in his life. It had never occurred to me that there could be a white man that did not enjoy the privilege of domination, but there it was. Joseph was closer to me than I was, if you catch my drift. He was right. I had been looking at the downside of this world for so long that even when there was an upside I never saw it. That need not make me a fool. I know the downside is bigger, but it is seeing the upside that keeps us moving in the direction of the good life. I give him one of those knowing forever Sto: loh smiles. He gets it because there is on one his face coming back at me. Joseph and me will be friends forever.

He describes the scene in the minutest detail and ends with, "It was amazing, man. It was amazing."

Wit speaks up, "Well, I guess I shall get to experience it first-hand. My little cousin wishes to participate and I have the privilege of being her chaperone in case the evil Will gets any ideas about her honour."

"Oooh," from Thomas.

"Painful," from Paul who has obviously seen her.

"What?" from Joseph who has not? I leave them to prattling on about the lovely Lei-Lani. Wit is at the center of the discourse on her virtues and her interest in me.

I am wandering off in my head, imagining my mom leaning out the window listening to Pop's flute music, next to her is Gramma. The longer the music plays the closer the two women get. At the tail end of the plaintive flute song the women both lean into the music. Mom imagines life with Pop. They take stock of him. He's old time. That's good. He is respectful in a Sto: loh way, but assertive, not shy, not young but definitely not fragile. Gramma knows his family. "They are hard working people," she whispers to her daughter. "The major virtue of the Sto: loh nation has become hard work." Gramma's generation turned it into a virtue. That was all they heard, lived, watched in the generation preceding.

Gramma is a little girl, she is picking her way through debris in the old landfill site, looking for old bikes with some usable parts left; a wheel here, a handlebar there, a steering column, a body and an axle. Bit by bit she assembles herself a bike. She gets on and wobbles her way across the dusty gravel road. She falls, skins her knees, bites back the stinging pain, and gets on again. She learns to ride. Now she can work.

She cleans the parish for the local priest. Her mom goes with her sometimes. The Priest never knows when Gramma's mother is going to be there, so he leaves her to her business. He scolds her often if she forgets something, but every week he pays her a quarter. She saves this money.

In the summer she heads for the hopyards with her Momma. They work twelve hour days. Gramma is at the top of the trellis; Great Gramma is below her. They pick flowers and pass them down to one another. At night on Friday, they cycle to town. On the roadway I see them ditch their bikes into the bush every time they see headlights or horses coming round the bend. I cringe. I know what that is about. They wear coveralls, scarves and binders.

My mind is drawn back to where I really am; the cafeteria. I get up to leave. I feel so sick. The food is speeding around in my belly so fast I am afraid I won't make it to the bathroom.

In the bathroom, as lunch leaves my body I come to understand the coveralls, Mac shirts and scarves covering their eyebrows; the women had to disguise themselves as men to be safe. Rape was so common back then. I really did not wish to know this. I lean against the stall asking Great Grandpa why I have to know all this. I close my eyes and he joins me, leaning against the other side of the stall.

"You don't have to know this," he answers, then closes his own eyes, "Neither did I, neither did my wife or my daughter, but it helped to know. It kept them safe." He disappears.

Hard work was about survival. It translated itself into cultural maxims. The scarf was about another kind of survival; it too translated itself into a cultural maxim. I see my cousins decked out in pretty dresses, hair done up, makeup on and I wonder if the old ladies envy that freedom. I wonder if the girls feel for that and I see why Mom's eyes have that far away sadness behind even her brightest smile and now I have to read those damn diaries.

I clean up and return to the lunch table.

"You look like you just saw a ghost," Wit says.

"I am sick," I say.

"Go home," Paul says, "We'll let the instructor know."

"Paul, you have no idea where I live, do you?" and Thomas and Wit laugh.

"Hey, I'll drive you," Joseph offers without a moments hesitation.

"Sure." And we are off and away. I want something funny to happen. I want to ask somebody some dumb question. I want to be the butt of a joke, just to relieve myself of the pressure of facing the history of our private world with these people. Joseph's voice is nipping at my silence; shredding the one moment I have before arriving at home to gather myself together. My blood is heating up. It feels like it is about to boil. I am seeing double and the world outside is spinning.

I wake up in a clean white hospital room, my mom looking down at me.

"What the?"

"Be still, you are one sick little puppy."

"What happened?"

"You passed out in Joseph's car. He brought you here."

The nurse comes into the room and tells my mom, "Well,

his A&D tests came back negative, but the doctor still wants to do a few other tests." The nurse turns and leaves.

"Joseph tried to convince them you were not drinking." Mom shrugs.

I am not going to be here long, so I determine not to argue with anyone about it, though it is maddening. I just lay here. The room starts to swim again. The nurse comes in, sees me hanging over the side of the bed, Mom's hand is ringing the bell. She pages the doctor who comes running.

"The doctor believes it's a ruptured appendix," I hear them telling my mom as she fades out of my view.

There is a nurse racing the wheeled bed down a hallway. I am leaning over the side, some candy striper is holding a metal bowl, trying real hard to catch what is left in my gut. I am moaning in pain between heaves, holding my side as another nurse is hooking me up to an intravenous. We are waiting at the elevator, the doctor is firing orders and someone is taking my blood pressure. In the elevator a nurse gives me a shot of something and there is something cool dripping into my veins. The elevator and all those white-clothed humans take another whirl in my eyes and I am gone.

Time collapses. It folds itself small. It floats into space, the black space between sound, smells and pictures. Lavender and the lusty voice of Josie wraps itself around me between two perfectly thick black wedges of timeless space. In the space is pain, deep and textured hot, then cold, then murky and dark. Rosewater. I know that smell. That's my mom's scent, it wafts out from between the spaces in the loose soft folds of her skirt. I hang on to the skirt, focus on the rose-water scent. The trellis comes into view. It sneaked right up and out from the black edges around her warm body and the touch of her hand on my forehead. Click, click, dip, trickle and a cool cloth touches my forehead. "Hush Willie." It's Callie, her long fingernails click, click, clicking as she soaks a cloth and wipes my forehead. I feel like Jesus on the cross in severe pain, except there are a whole army of women dabbing the sweat from my brow. They are all whispering that I can make it. "Fight for yourself, boy, push back from death's door, come on, Will, only the good die young." In the slimmest wedge of light between the dark spaces I hear men's mumbles. They never know what to say in circumstances like this so they kind of grunt their way through it. They don't do anything useful much either, but I am kind of glad they showed up. It must be late.

"Weren't we doing something?" I ask.

"Boy, you got to learn to look without gapping so seriously." It is Josie. The words come out sticky and serious. She means for me to swallow them. I do. Her fingers, though stricken with arthritis, are running through my hair. Someone is rolling me over. This means another of those damn needles in my backside. I want to tell them to back off, but the room is swimming from bright light on its outer edges. Fading and whirling, the dark outer edges consume the center and finally I am sailing between the wedges of light and dark again.

I am short, so short I can't see the counter top. I have a nickel in my hand. There is a friendly sounding voice at the other end of the counter, but I can't see it. Some hands

lift me. There she is, it's Winnie taking my nickel and giving me a chocolate bar. I chuckle. A chocolate bar must cost
somewhere near a dollar.

"Thanks Winnie."

"It's me, Willie, Jay," she says. I roll my eyes in her
direction. The effort is too much; the black puffball of dark
surrounding joy is spongy and it wipes me up, soaks up my
awareness and delivers me to sleep. The sounds between
the wedges are getting louder, the wedges are shrinking into
slivers and then they finally disappear.

I am really dreaming now, not floating between life and
death. I dream these women take turns wiping my forehead.
I see them, wiping up messes I have made forever. They
never grow tired of wiping my forehead, my hands, my feet
and my illness. They surround me with soft cloth, sweet
scents, tasty treats and gentle voices. They call me, out of
bed, away from the TV when I sit too close, off the road
when I endanger myself, to school when I need to know and
now, they call me from death's dark edges. I smile at their
voices; drink in their different perfumes, relish the sounds
they make. Each one seems so different and each one seems
so the same.

I am still smiling when I wake up, this time it is a serious
wake up.

"Look, his eyes are open," my little niece tells everyone. They move forward slowly afraid that I will drift away
again. I don't. They get ready to laugh, to release this terrible tension of trying to will me to live.

"Uncle, you almost died." Someone says it like it was the
very worst thing I had ever pulled on them.

I laugh and grab my side; the pain shoots through me, but doesn't give me any inclination to sleep.

"Drugs... I want drugs." The room cracks up.

The nurse enters. "Okay, if you guys are going to get him laughing, I am going to chase all of you, but two, out of here." The nurse tells me, "No laughing, you have a lot of stitches, so no laughing." They all suck wind and hold till she leaves, then they crack up. I really try not to.

Callie's little boy moves close to my face. He is so cute, just started talking in full sentences over the past month or so. I have no idea what he is going to say, but I am really waiting and listening hard for it, because I know it is going to be nearly un-understandable.

"Wheah iss it?" He asks secretively, holding his hand over his lips like he is prepared to maintain confidence.

Callie mouths, "Where is it?"

"My appendix?" I ask him with the same amount of secrecy.

"Yes," he says.

"They threw it away." He starts to cry. No one has any clue why he is crying. He can't talk enough to tell us. When the nurse comes in he leans over and tries to rake her face screaming, "Give back!" I am trying desperately not to laugh. The nurse backs up, she must be thinking the baby has gone berserk.

Callie is laughing, assuring him I don't need the appendix; it was no good, so they gave me stitches instead. This quiets him.

"Wheah?"

"Good move, Callie. Where?" Josie teases.

"Under my bandage?" I offer. They all look at me spitting steel. "No?"

"Wheah?" I open the sheet and show him the bandage.

"Oh," he says and remembered he attacked the nurse and turned to her to say, "sorry." Even the nurse laughs.

"Don't laugh. All of you stop!" Callie's little girl puts up both her hands and looks at the floor, her face registers threat.

"If you don't stop making poor Uncle Will laugh I am going to get mad." Callie decides to take her darlings home.

"So what happened?" I ask my mom.

"Well, it appears your appendix ruptured. You almost died. Grandpa sang every night. The men joined him. The doctors didn't think you'd make it, but we knew you would."

There must be so much more than that. I don't believe I will get a good clean version of what happened. They won't tell me that they stayed up all night and day with me, and breathed shards of tension in every time I looked like I was going over the edge. They won't talk about how they held their breath each time I looked like I was leaving for good. They won't tell me about all their little attentions, the wiping of the sweat from my brow, the sitting for hours and hours telling me to fight to come back. Oh hell, I know what happened.

I imagine every woman in my family took turns sitting by my bedside. When they weren't by my side; they were slogging gravel at the daycare. They crooned, they sang and they cajoled, each of them pushing their own strength through their fingers and hoping my skin would pick it up and pull me through it. They prayed silently in their minds while they dug, hammered, and cooked. They sent words of encouragement to the men who went to sing for me. They cooked, cleaned and mopped up after the singing was over. They flopped into bed and rose again to repeat it all every day until I woke up. There was so much more than that too.

Their emotional heartstrings were stretched beyond belief. Even while their love was stretched thin they managed to send out encouraging words to the other family members, they found time to laugh, to hug, to kiss, to clean the dust off themselves and to love.

The tears are rolling down my face when Josie strolls in. She takes my hand and tosses her head the way she does. I breath out, but not hard. I know it'll hurt to make a sound.

"Thanks Josie."

She smiles, and pats the back of my hand like it was pure. "Got some other visitors when you are ready." She reaches for a Kleenex and wipes my eyes. "You ready?"

"Yeah."

Lei-Lani and her mother stroll in. "Ha-ay," I say, just like a hundred other men in my lineage have said before me. Lei-Lani's mother tells me I scared everyone. I apologize.

"That definitely is not my intent with you and your daughter, Ms. Jacobs," I say and wink. She laughs.

Anne is behind Lani. They visit, each one asking some question about what I might need. There is a small space of quiet in the room.

"I know what I need." They lean forward slightly. "The date. I need to know what day it is."

"Friday, one week from when this all began. You missed your birthday, Bud." It is Sarah coming out from behind Lani.

"Ha-ay," I breath deep and easy.

The nurse returns with a needle; she looks at everyone. They say goodnight, promise to return tomorrow and leave. I look out the window at Gramma Moon. She looks like she's smiling. This time there are no black spaces, just a gentle drift in sleep.

Chapter 16

At first, I think that morning has come. At least it feels like morning. But it is still dark. It is middle of the night morning. In exactly two weeks, my life has become insane. The movies in my mind I used to see in the moonlight at night have started sneaking up on me during the day.

Before this happened my mom handed me a stack of journals I am afraid to read. I know what's in them. I am not even sure how I know. I heard of Residential School. We all have. Maybe the newspapers, maybe hushed conversations wafting from the kitchen, voices from women trying to decide whether they should remember, what they would do if they tried to remember, what others are doing about remembering. I have heard the word "healing" hundreds of times in my life. Next to "sobriety" this word seems to dominate any woman who is sober and not being beat up. I have no idea what they really mean. No one has beat me up or been drunk or abusive around me, although there is plenty of opportunity in my community to subject myself to that. I saw the TV announcement of the government to the Indians on healing from Residential School. As usual, it is a granting system, which means the village gets to apply for money—to do what?

My mom said she was angry all the time she was there. She had gripped the wheel so tight that her hands changed colour. What made her think I was interested? How did she get that from my conversation with Josie? I was just picking up on some curious remark Josie made. I am sure I want to be an environmental scientist. Is this Residential School history, the story of hard work of my Great Grandma and Grandpa I saw in the moonlight a cultural imperative connected to that? The Wit thing seems so small compared to all this. I have just alienated the most knowledgeable man in the Sto: loh Nation. I need to know something here. If I could only figure out the question, it would help.

Lei-Lani said something. What was it? Something about some novelist, a woman, a writer, who knows something about First Nation's science and something about Western science. It is all becoming a series of fast moving twisted snakes tying themselves in knots in the pits they have established in my mind when the nurse comes in.

"Good morning, how are you?"

"Well," I start, "I am missing a body part, there is a crack in my gut about six inches long, I am still foggy from drugs you gave me and it is too early for the sun to be up. I missed my birthday whirling about on a drug induced toxic dream ride and I am a confused teenager who has gone and ticked off, Buster-Jesus-Christ-second-coming, the only person in the world who might save me from my confusion."

"Wow." There is a pause, and she replies, "I cannot replace your body. I can clean the crack in your gut. I have no idea what you're all fogged up about. I do remember being a teenager. I remember being fogged up myself. To my recollection the fog did lift. Let's have a look?"

It is my turn to say, "Wow." I lift my shirt. She opens the bandage from underneat, so I can't see it, although I am looking.

"You may not want to see this," she says.

I managed to remain still. I receive the pain. It rushes to my head, which makes my eyes water, but my stomach muscles do not wince and my mouth stays shut.

"Pretty good." The nurse is properly impressed.

"I am a guy. Guys like blood and gore," I tell her while still trying to look.

"Not usually their own," she smiles.

I twist my face every which way trying to hold back a laugh on that one.

"Score," I squeeze out. She laughs. I breathe out. She allows me to see.

There it is. It is puffed up pretty good. It doesn't look all that closed, which means the scar will be magnificent. It looks like it's more than six inches long.

"Why is it so big? If my science book was right my appendix is about an inch long. Does it mean the doc didn't really have a clue where it was and needed a big hole to hunt it down?"

She laughs only slightly at the thought, then answers somewhat facetiously, "Traditionally, doctors try to make the biggest scars possible in male teenagers. Boys, they believe, thrive better with horrendous scars, some sort of throwback from the caveman days."

I cannot resist a chuckle on that one. I wince.

"Sorry. That isn't it at all. Your appendix ruptured. They initially went in with a smaller cut, saw it was ruptured and opened you up wide to try and remove as much of the infection from your abdomen as possible and to find the now itty bitty little appendix which sometimes flies around that empty cavity when it bursts."

I have no idea why that strikes me as funnier than her joke, but it does. This thing pops like a balloon goes zinging around in an empty space and lands who knows where. A bunch of white guys in uniforms, all masked up are poking and prodding trying to find the busted balloon.

"Which goes to show life don't change much no matter how grown-up you get."

"Excuse me?"

"I remember doing that with balloons, blowing them up, letting them go, and then a bunch of us kids hunting them down," she howls.

"Well, that's one way of looking at it."

"It's because I am a teenager."

She looks completely caught off guard. Josie wouldn't be. She would pick up that piece from the earlier conversation just like she knew it was the second dance in the whirl around the circle of my confusion.

"The confusion?"

"Oh, the second part of your monologue on how you're doing this morning. Being a teenager and being confused are synonymous. What is important is how you deal with it. Are you thinking about suicide at all?"

"Over confusion. People commit suicide over confusion?"

"People commit suicide over a lot of things. Sometimes attempts are the only way kids think they are going to get heard. They attempt suicide but don't necessarily wish to die. Sometimes it's a cry for help," she says. There is a trace of sadness in her eyes.

"That is some serious crying. Well, I have been fairly successful at everything I have ever attempted, so that would not be a good way for me to cry out to get heard. With my luck I would succeed. There are a few things I would like to accomplish before my journeys end." I list them in my mind. Sex is pretty close to the top. I decline telling this to the young lady. But clarity is right behind that.

So I tell the nurse, "Clarity about some of the things running through my head would help make the journey to the other side smoother."

She gives me a look. It has a smile in it, a kind of pride in meeting someone you kind of want to know and an "I know what you mean" kind of look.

"You, my friend will not be confused long." She bandages the wound and leaves towards the door.

Now she is a nice lady, but that last remark has a cheerleader kind of quality to it that really doesn't help. I feel like I am losing the game and the other guys have me tossed in a confused tailspin and I can't figure out which play is going to get me to stop chasing my tail.

"Hey, nurse," I call out to her just before she disappears from sight.

"Yes?"

"How long will I be here?"

"Your chart says ten days. Trust me. You will need every one. They usually send you home too soon." And she is gone.

"Great, ten days to think, if I knew how to do that, the ten days might be useful. So far all my thinking has got me tied up in some pretty big knots." No one is awake so saying this out loud doesn't hurt or benefit anyone. I turn my head just in time to see the sun creeping up on the skyline. My window must be in the eastern doorway. That at least is a bonus.

I am not in my own room, so no tobacco to ask that eastern sun for some wisdom here. If I ask for some they will likely think I want to smoke, that is against the law. Oh, wait a minute. I am sixteen now. Relax, Will, you have a lot of days to lay out tobacco. As soon as visiting hours start the troupe of relatives will arrive—plenty of time.

Hmm, that's a new one. First time I ever argued with myself. What's up with that? Don't start giving yourself questions. Hey, do you think this is a new me surfacing?

The snakes unravel. On their backs are written all kinds of craziness: there is a diamond back with 'Wit the Homo' written on it, a common gardener with Buster-Jesus-Christ-second-coming, a cobra with Residential School, a boa constrictor with 'healing and sobriety' on it, and an anaconda with 'environmental science' on it. My muscles feel quivery; my leg is twitching mid-thigh. I look under the covers. It is visible, this twitch. My breath is getting short. The snakes crawl about, some slow, some fast, over each other, under around and about. I can't breathe. My forehead is breaking out in a cold sweat. I am slipping into panic mode, when breakfast arrives. Breakfast is a new bag for my IV tree. The nurse checks my temperature and rings the bell. I pass out. My parting thought is, if the rest of the journey to manhood is going to be like this, suicide might start to look good.

Chapter 18

I wake up a little later.

"We are having some trouble with the antibiotic," I hear a doctor telling my mother, who is in the hall just outside the room. "He seems to have some sort of allergy to it." That is a relief. I thought I was going mad.

"What is this, a crap shoot? You give him medicine that poisons him, then try another!" Gramma asks the doctor.

Good going Gramma, you tell them! Of course, they are medical practitioners; just too bad they have to practise on me.

"That is pretty much it," the young doctor admits. I picture him turning red, feeling guilty, then he adds, "We are going to keep him in intensive care so he can be on twenty-four hour watch." There is a pause.

"How long?" The tense tired words by a voice that just wants to cry comes from my mom. I hurt when she does. I don't know how to describe it, but it's kind of heavy. I just wish it were someone else causing her this pain.

"Until the infection clears up. He is okay for now, but we have him here just to be on the safe side." A body rises from the chair next to my bed. I didn't know anyone was here with me. She puts the book she is reading down and starts changing the IV.

"I won't be putting on any weight with meals like this." She smiles. She is Black, she moves languid and slow.

"For sure." She says with an accent you never hear on television. "My name is Toni," she tells me. I want to ask her where she is from, but that seems like an Indian thing. I don't know if it is all that important to Black people, so I don't.

"You have an accent." I venture.

"West Indian," she responds, "It's what happens when a bunch of Celtic speaking white men, Caribbean Indians and who-knows-what-speaking Africans mix it all up in English."

"How long you been sitting there?"

"About two hours. You have been out for about four. Your folks are waiting, do I call them in?" I nod. Great, I will be convalescing here with an audience. My family will not be satisfied with just a nurse watching over me; they shall deploy the women in my family to cover the visiting hours at least and I shall have a nurse all the time.

"He's awake, if you want to talk to him."

Instead of coming in the room they leave with the doctor.

"Where are they going?" I ask.

"To get masks and gowns. They will be back two at a time." I already know the lineup. It is the secret hierarchy of my family. Mom and Gramma first, then Pop and Tony,

Pop and Grandpa if Grandpa came, George and Callie and maybe Thomas, Josie will be by herself, then Anne and Sarah. I will have a fifteen minute uncomfortable audience with each one in which we will all try to drum up conversation about the crisis but will strictly avoid any talking about the feelings we are all repressing during this crisis. We will come close to tears then swallow hard or breathe out and make that sound, but we will definitely not be saying how scared we all are.

"Don't worry son. We will be here around the clock. This won't happen again."

"Funny thing, Mom, I wasn't worried. I have no idea why. I guess I really believe you only leave this earth when you have done what you came here to do." I can't believe the words dropping from my lips.

"You know what I really like about being your son?" Her eyes open wide with shock. "I love the love. Loving women all my life have surrounded me. When I started all this becoming a man stuff though, I was told I would have to make decisions alone. I have ten days of alone time. It is a gift. But if you all are here I will miss out on that gift, so I would really rather you didn't do that. I have some things on my mind. Could you just visit me once a day and bring me those books I left in the truck? You know the ones I am talking about." The air in the room got still.

"Yes, yes I can do that." She fiddles with my sheets, then quietly leaves. I know she is going to cry. Maybe she needs too. But I need this time alone. Gramma smiles at me. I can do no wrong. I want her to disappear and she just treats it like the happiest piece of luck she has ever had.

"You behave yourself around all them pretty nurses" quips and she is out the door. Pop and Tony are next.

"That's good son," Pop says, Mom already told hi

"Though I believe your mom will worry."

"She is going to worry anyway," Tony offers. "She th on it. Why if she didn't have you to worry about, she make one up."

"Or create one," and we chuckle. I try to hold the up in my face away from my gut.

"You need anything?"

"Books. Not school books though, real ones. Ones will tell me about us, about Residential School, about ronmental science, about self-government, nationhood. books."

"We can do that," Tony says. Pop looks at him like surprised we can, but doesn't argue. They leave. Sarah Josie are next.

"Where are George and Callie?"

"Digging," Josie says, and they both laugh.

"Callie's trying to do your share."

"TMI," I tell her, "too much information," I explai Josie.

"Could you get me that book from that writer you w talking about and I want one about Residential School by Indian if you can?" I ask Sarah.

"Sure," Sarah says. "We were all so scared, Will. T is twice now in a week someone has called to say you n not make it. Your mom jumps every time she hears phone."

"You know what Sarah. I can't do anything about my mom's fear. I can't do much about yours either except to say find your courage. If anything happens to me, I'll see you on the other side forever and that's a mighty long time. I don't mean to sound cold, but I got all these things called emotions running around, attached to crazy looking loose snakes and I haven't been able to do much about them either. So what am I supposed to do about someone else's old snakes."

"You could tell her not to be scared," Sarah's voice is pouting.

"She has to express that fear first. You and I both know she isn't about to do that. I can't guess that she is afraid. Remember: 'don't speculate what's going on in someone else's mind boy, you don't get to name Sarah's feelings.' I remember. Mom hollered that at me when I said I didn't hurt you that bad."

"I'm surprised you remember that."

"I am too. No, actually, I remember a whole lot of things. What I don't like is remembering them. I am going to live by them for a while, to see if they work. You know what I mean, Sarah? We get all this 'Sto: loh's are this way and that way,' but we don't think about whether it works all the time. Half the time we are running in a frenzy like the rest of the world, lawless, and the rest of the time we are bending and stretching the law to suit ourselves in the moment. I don't want to do that. I figure I will live with them, see how they really sit with me, then decide whether I want to hang on to them."

"You're a scary boy, Will." Josie is about to try and talk me out of it. Guilt will be her major weapon. I close up. She sees me closing up and changes her mind. "I suppose we should retire and muster up the courage to live with this scary boy, Sarah." They lean forward, kiss my forehead and depart.

"You're much too serious for a teenager," the nurse says.

"The world is not serious enough for a simple thing called peace," I answer.

"Um-um," she says, "You want to solve the world's problems?"

"No. I just don't want to be adding to them. I want to be serious enough for peace."

"You have no idea how hard that is or how much you need to know to make that happen."

"True, but if I live as long as my grandpa, and I will do my best to live that long, I have sixty-nine years of trying left. There are 3,650 days in a decade. That means I have 30,000 days, give or take a few hundred to figure that out. There are twenty-four hours in a day. I sleep out eight. I will likely work eight either at school or at a job. I will probably be a friend, father, husband or uncle or son for six hours a day. That leaves me two hours a week for 30,000 days or 1,153 hours to find out the knowledge I need to figure it out."

"Wow, that was some fast math. I get it," she says, "This here ten days will be the longest stretch you are going to have in one block and you don't want to waste."

"Thanks, I was thinking that. I was busying trying to multiply 1,153 x 60 to figure out how many minutes that would be, but you know what I'm trying to say."

"I know. My head was beginning to hurt with all that calculating going on in your mind, so I stopped you." She hands me a pen. "Go ahead, complete the process. It is good to see a young man who knows something about something." She laughs, sets herself down and picks up a brand new book from out of her bag and begins to read.

"What are you reading?" I ask.

"Jazz," she says.

"What's it about?"

"Me, my mother, my grandmother, my pop, my children, my today and all my yesterdays. From it, I plan to figure out my tomorrows. You want to hear some of it?" I nod 'yes.'

"Ts. I know that woman..." She reads for a long time. The words are like a song with the rhythm always changing; the landscape of this island haunted by city sidewalks like a lonely flute song. I play with the sound of it in my mind. She gets to the part about the Iroquois sky and I think about the purple in it. There is no purple in my skyline. It makes me want to go to New York. Iroquois. There is a sound in those words that calls us all to attention even out here in this tiny Sto: loh world.

"The people who always have their coats off, drop their blankets in a minute." I hear my grandpa's voice. The nurse puts the book down. Grandpa sits in a chair and tells her to go on.

"Grandpa, I would..."

"I'm blind, not deaf, your mom told me." He wiggles

his cane, signaling the nurse to go on. She looks from him to me. I nod. She reads till her voice starts to rasp, drinks some water, reads some more. I drift over the life of this woman, this young girl, this man, their ancestors running from slavery.

I see a Cree man on horseback in a dense thicket. There are people running in his direction. The runners are Black people—two men and a woman. The Cree man has two horses tethered to the tree next to him. The two men climb on the back of a horse and the Cree lifts the woman onto his. No saddle. The Black guys aren't so good with the horse, but the Cree shows them how to move it forward, left and right. He hands them a bag of pemmican. They do their best to follow this Indian in the dark with no moonlight; they pick their way through the bush. All three horses are dragging buffalo beans broom flowers weighted with horse-shoes. The brooms are sweeping their tracks behind them. Sunlight breaks and they hide in the thickets till dark and off they go again. No conversation takes place. They hide by day, ride by night, until they get to the Cree guy's village. He points them north and the three of them carry on.

Iroquois sky parts. There is a dock. Thousands of men tied and tethered together are moving in a slow staggering line toward a ship. They cut the tether every three-hundred men, then cut their hair off and load them in the ship. The ship leaves. They bring around a bucket of slop and hold a ladle full to each mouth, some drink the slop, and some don't. The guy with the slop bucket moves on.

Another ship comes. Another 300 are cut loose. Days go on. Those who refuse to eat are lying on the ground in the mud under the sky, watching its purple drift over their last dreams here on earth as they lay dying. Another ship, another three hundred and the dead are culled as they board. The others dare not urge the dying to choose another path. They stay quiet, sing sad old songs, tell jokes, tell stories, but never tell the men to eat. 7,000 Cree men head for the West Indies under the pale glow of an Iroquois sky.

Alongside the slaves running north, between the paths cut by the night train to freedom are the women who once shared their lives with these men. They are being herded north away from the prairie they know. They are beyond grief. They don't even have the bones of their men to carry, there is no body to grieve, and they have no idea where these men have gone. They stumble; some die in the cold, grief-filled days as the American army herds them north— north to where they don't know. They know there are Cree up there, they have met them, but they are not related to any of them. There will be no one to hunt for them, no one to built their homes for them, no one to keep their bodies warm at night, no one to give them more children, to bury them, to marry them; their lives have ground to a screeching halt. There is no story to guide them, no previous experience to rely upon, to govern their possible response.

"We are salmon people," Grandpa interjects, "not cotton people." He treats the passage about the cotton fields in the book as a metaphor for the way Black people in America are and I don't know enough about them to know whether or not he is right, but his comment sets me to wondering. Maybe he is right. Maybe this spiked-sharp-cotton-boll tells more about them than anything else. Maybe he is so wrong.

Maybe the chains of slavery tell more about the cotton boll than that cotton tells about the people. It doesn't matter. He is about to tell a story and I am about to listen along with this Black, Caribbean, and Celtic, possibly Cree, nurse.

Salmon people. A woman leaps, is pushed by a man. He leaps, crashes, leaps again, and makes it. Another pair join the hundreds of us that are there in that pool together. After a mating pair makes it, another pair eases themselves into the pool and follows them. I can hear the pairs in the pool and along the river's edge encouraging each other, urging their relatives to jump. Every man among them will make this leap without the benefit of a push up, but they are never completely by themselves. Their male and female relatives surround them. The only one standing alone is the mate of the jumper waiting in an eddy just up and over the falls.

I am at the bottom of the falls. I can see the river. The stretch of river behind me is lined with my siblings and their mates, nuzzling, watching and waiting for me to jump. I heave my woman over the falls. I swim in crazy circles, jump willfully, listen for some piece of advice about acquiring the agility and the strength to succeed from some relative, then swim again and leap again. I break my spine, gash my sides, and nearly kill myself getting over those falls. I arrive in this little eddy cradling my mate. I can almost see her smile. The story is clear. Women are about imagining future, and men are about helping women so they can imagine future. Grandpa's voice is mesmerizing. The words coming out are forever words, 'spiritual language' we say nowadays.

Grandpa knows something about something. I laugh.

"I get it."

When I get home I will ask my folks to hold a feast for those Cree men. I determine to ask Grandpa to lay out tobacco for this nurse; this gal, Toni, who helped me get it. This last thought brings me peace. I slip from the room and retreat into dreaming. I know I am going to be okay.